Prologue

October 15, 1888

Two days have passed since Mother died. The neighbors do not come by to pay their respects. I watch them hurry past our house and shiver, as if the misery here were like a cold hand pressing them away from our front gate.

My thoughts remain entirely on that fatal night. It sticks in my mind like a nightmare too horrible for any detail to be forgotten.

The house was quiet. It was so still and peaceful that I could feel the gentle pulsing of the waves on the shoreline almost a quarter of a mile away. The cats were sleeping by the fire. Then Mother came rushing in. She was naked, and her hair was wild.

"Máirín," she cried, her eyes glistening, "it is done."

I had experienced far too many strange nights since Mother had been ill to be completely shocked. Calmly, so as not to frighten her away, I crossed the room to cover her. When I got close, however, I saw that her hands were covered in blood. She had pricked both of her thumbs, and there were smears of blood all over her body. To be skyclad and to show signs of letting one's own blood—these are signs of the darkest magick. This was not something I had encountered before.

"What have you done?" I gasped.

She reached up and began gently stroking my face in reply. As I tried to put the blanket over her shoulders, she ran away from me, up the stairs. She moved with unnatural power and speed. As she ran, I heard her yelling out. She was spelling, that I knew, but her voice was crazed and unintelligible.

I had no time to take a lamp to guide me, and I stumbled up the dark steps after her. I found her on the widow's walk, on her knees, calling out to the moon in words I could not recognize. She went limp as I approached and seemed to lose interest in whatever it was she was doing, and I had a terrible feeling that she had just had time to complete whatever it was. Again I begged her to tell me what she had done.

"Soon," she said, "soon you'll know."

She allowed me to lead her back downstairs, where I washed away the blood and dressed her in a nightgown. She kept calling her own name over and over again, "Oona . . . Oona . . ." dragging the words along in a pitiful moan until the act of repetition exhausted her.

When I came back to the parlor, I passed by the glass and saw myself. On my face, sketched out in blood, were hexing signs—

Book Thirteen

sweep

Cate Tiernan

RECKONING

speak

An Imprint of Penguin Group (USA) Inc.

Reckoning

SPEAK

Published by the Penguin Group
Penguin Group (USA) Inc., 345 Hudson Street, New York, New York 10014, U.S.A.
Penguin Group (Canada), 90 Eglinton Avenue East, Suite 700, Toronto, Ontario M4P 2Y3, Canada
(a division of Pearson Penguin Canada Inc.)
Penguin Books Ltd, 80 Strand, London WC2R 0RL, England
Penguin Group (Australia), 250 Camberwell Road, Camberwell, Victoria 3124, Australia
(a division of Pearson Australia Group Pty Ltd)
Penguin Group (NZ), 67 Apollo Drive, Rosedale, North Shore 0632, New Zealand
(a division of Pearson New Zealand Ltd)
Penguin Books (South Africa) (Pty) Ltd, 24 Sturdee Avenue,
Rosebank, Johannesburg 2196, South Africa

Published by Puffin Books, a division of Penguin Young Readers Group, 2002
This edition published by Speak, an imprint of Penguin Group (USA) Inc., 2009

5   7   9   10   8   6   4

Cover Photography copyright © 2001 Barry David Marcus
Photo-illustration by Marci Senders
Series Design by Russell Gordon

Produced by 17th Street Productions,
an Alloy company
151 West 26th Street
New York, NY 10001

17th Street Productions and associated logos
are trademarks and/or registered trademarks of Alloy, Inc.

ISBN 978-0-14-241028-8

Printed in the United States of America

www.penguin.com

that's what she had been doing when she touched me. Horrified, I ran to the basin of seawater that I kept in the kitchen for scrying and washed them away as quickly as I could. I stayed up half the night, trying to dispel whatever it was that she had done. I burned rosemary and uttered every purification and deflection spell I'd ever learned.

The next morning her bed was empty.

A fisherman found her yesterday. She was about half a mile from the house, washed up on the shore. She had gone out during the night and walked into the water. She still wore her nightgown.

Now the house shudders. This morning the windows broke for no reason. The mirror in the parlor cracked from side to side.

Mighty Goddess, guide her spirit and have mercy on me, her daughter. May I break my voice, lose it forever from my lamentations and weeping. My mother, Oona Doyle of Ròiseal, is gone, and something dark has come in her stead.

—Máirín

1

Omens

June 14, 1942

The ghosts are angry today. They smashed a vase in the front room, and they knocked over a lamp. The lamp almost hit our cat, Tady. He ran and hid under the sofa. Mother told us to be brave and not to cry, so I have been trying very hard. I have not cried once, even though the ghosts started banging the door of my room open and shut. My little sister, Tioma, is not as brave as I am. She hid in her closet and sobbed. She does not understand that we must prove to the ghosts that we are not afraid. That is the only way we can get them to leave.

—Aoibheann

Finally, some peace and quiet.

Hilary, my father's girlfriend, is pregnant. Since she'd moved in a few weeks before, I had been more or less treated like a pet or a piece of furniture, just something to be dealt with or moved around while they were getting ready for the "real" child to come.

Among her many awful ideas, Hilary had major redecoration plans. These included taking up a lot of the carpet, painting all the walls in a color called "aubergine dream" (also known as "scary purple"), and putting our sofa into some kind of big white bag. My father was letting her redecorate to her heart's content, and I had to stand back and watch as everything familiar to me vanished. Despite my protests, she'd recruited me to help. All of my free time seemed to be spent helping Hilary with her painting, her relentless scrapbooking, and the wedding plans. It was like being forced to dig my own grave.

But tonight—a reprieve. They'd decided to go out and see a movie. I *lived* for nights like this one, when they were out of the house. I was supposed to be doing my homework, but I had to savor the time I had on my own. It was far too precious to waste. So instead of doing math, I watched reruns of *Buffy the Vampire Slayer*. When I heard the car pull into the driveway, I switched off the TV and pulled my algebra book into my lap—the classic I've-been-studying-all-night trick. No one falls for it, but everyone tries it, anyway.

The door opened, and my dad came in making faces and talking *baby talk* to Hilary, and of course she was baby talking right back. It was probably the most awful thing I'd ever seen in my entire life, and let me tell you, I'd seen some bad stuff recently. When they turned and saw me gaping in horror, they looked genuinely surprised.

"You're home . . ." my dad said, suddenly looking embarrassed. "You're up."

Well, hello? It was nine o'clock on a Wednesday. Where did he think I'd be?

"Yeah," I said, reaching for a pencil, which I was considering using to poke out my eyes so I wouldn't have to witness any more of this unbearable cuteness. "Just doing my homework."

"Have you cleaned out your room yet?" Hilary asked.

"No."

"You know we have to get it ready," she said, dropping her spreading butt onto the bagged couch and picking through her crocheting.

Another sore point. Because it was next to my dad's—or *their* room—Hilary had set her sights on turning my bedroom into a nursery. She wanted to move me to the little room at the end of the hall.

"I'll do it when I have time," I said, suddenly finding my factoring exercises totally engrossing. "I have a quiz tomorrow."

"I know you don't want to switch rooms, Alisa," Hilary said with a sigh, "but when the baby comes, I'll need to be able to get to him or her quickly in the middle of the night. This is as much for you as it is for me. The room at the end of the hall will be less noisy."

She had to be kidding. The room at the end of the hall was a glorified closet. In fact, it wasn't even glorified. It was pure, plain closet. It had a tiny window, too small for normal blinds or curtains. It was more like a vent. I looked to my dad for support, but he just folded his arms over his chest.

"Hilary's been asking you about this for over a week now," he said, getting into his stern voice.

"I said that I'll do it," I replied, trying to keep the anger out of my voice. Algebra never looked more appealing.

"You'll do it after school tomorrow," he said, "or you're in all weekend."

I definitely wasn't going to let myself get stuck in the house with Hilary. Rather than say something I would later regret, I nodded, grabbed my things, and got out of there as quickly as I could. At that moment Hilary's pregnancy scrapbook tumbled off the table, scattering photos and papers everywhere.

"Oh, no!" Hilary said, bending over to pick up the scattered contents. My dad swooped down to help her, and I left the room. Fortunately they had no idea I had anything to do with it. I hadn't meant to do it, either. These things just kind of happen to me. Objects fall off walls, fly across rooms, and tumble off tables when I'm around.

See, I'm half witch.

A few months ago I didn't know real witches existed. Even a month or so ago I had been terrified of magick, of Wicca, and of anyone who had anything to do with it. But everything had changed in the last couple of weeks, after I discovered my mother's Book of Shadows at Morgan Rowlands's house. I read it and realized that my mother had been a Rowanwand witch from Gloucester, Massachusetts. She was as afraid of her power as I was—so much so that she actually stripped herself of her magick in order to lead a normal life. She died when I was three, so she never had a chance to tell me this herself.

A blood witch is the child of two witches, descendants of the Seven Great Clans of Wicca. Since my father was a non-witch, I was only a half. Technically this meant that I wasn't supposed to have power. For some reason, I did—in abundance. To top it off, I had a whopping bad case of uncontrollable telekinesis. Even in witch terms, I was really strange. Because I was such an odd case, I was able to withstand the more serious effects of a dark wave spell that had been cast against our coven, Kithic, a few days before. While all of the other blood witches became incredibly ill, I got only a slight headache. I was strong enough to perform the spell that defeated the wave that would have killed all of the members of our coven and their families.

My father didn't know about any of this, and he certainly wouldn't have believed me if I had told him. He probably would have sent me to a therapist, claiming that I was making a really weird cry for attention.

Once safely in my room, I switched on my computer to check my e-mail. There was a note waiting for me from Mary K., Morgan's younger sister and my good friend.

> Hi, A.,
>
> What have you been up to? You seem kind of out of it lately. Anything wrong? We should hang out. Gimme a call or send me a note.
>
> —M. K.

I'd been wondering for a while what to do about Mary K. She's Catholic and completely turned off by Wicca. Just a couple of weeks before, I'd been trying to help her persuade Morgan to give up magick. Everything was different now. I was a witch; I had powers. And I'd seen the good that magick could do, how it could be used to fight evil.

I knew I'd have to tell her the truth at some point—that I was back in Kithic, that I was a Wiccan, that I was a blood witch. Mary K. was going to freak, there was no question about that. I was going to have to do it, anyway. I sent her off a note, suggesting that we meet after school at her house the next day to hang out. It was a ruse, of course. Devious me. I would have to think of some way to break the truth to her once I got there.

I switched off the computer and climbed into bed. I took out my mother's Book of Shadows and the collection of letters written to her by her brother, Sam. I paged through these every single night before going to sleep. It was reassuring. Here was her entry about Sam putting her bike up on the widow's walk of the house. Here was the one about looking at the lilacs in the window of the flower shop and the one about passing her driver's exam. Except for the magick parts, my mom's life sounded so nice and normal, so fun . . . until the later parts of the book, when her brother performed a spell that accidentally produced a deadly storm. I usually didn't read that far in. I stayed near the beginning.

Sighing, I put the book and the letters in a big pile by the side of my bed and turned over to go to sleep. A strange dream overtook me instantly.

The sky was yellowish green, pulsing with the energy of a storm about to break loose. I was on a rocky shore. There were buildings just behind me. This was a town, not a desolate stretch along the water. Somehow I understood at once that this was Gloucester, Massachusetts, my mother's hometown.

The weather had whipped the ocean into a frenzy. High, dangerous waves were crashing down just a few feet from where I stood. Any one of them could have snapped me up and taken me out to sea, killing me in a moment. Instead of running for cover, though, I was looking at something far down the beach—a woman, sitting calmly on a large rock, waving to me. I started to walk closer to her, and I could tell as I approached that she was not an ordinary woman. The top half of her body was normal, though unclothed. The bottom half of her body was a steel gray finned tail, which flicked and twitched whenever the water lapped against it. She was a mermaid.

The distance between us sometimes grew when I should have been getting closer. Finally I was just close enough to be able to see her face, but she spun around to hide herself with her long hair and dove straight into the water, vanishing from my sight. At the same moment a wave hung above my head, poised to crash down on me.

And I woke up. My alarm was going off.

Shivering, I crawled to the bathroom for a shower. The water reminded me of the rain shower on the beach, and I swore I could still feel the cool sand under my toes. I'd heard that witches' dreams could sometimes be very powerful. Sometimes they were signs, visions. I started to think about this.

I'd stumbled onto my mother's Book of Shadows: The chances were one in a million that it would turn up at Morgan's house, yet it had found its way to me. I'd discovered my uncle's letters that had been hidden for years in the trap compartment of my mother's old jewelry box. And now I was dreaming of Gloucester—and dreaming so vividly that I could taste the salty breeze. Sky Eventide, one of the blood witches in Kithic, always says that there are no coincidences. What if that was true? The things that had been happening to me were so strange, so unlikely. What if this was all a series of signs, telling me to do something?

Like what?

Well, there was my uncle, Sam Curtis, for a start. I hadn't even known I had an uncle. But now I'd found the letters, and now I knew he existed. I also knew he loved my mother. Maybe he would want to know about me. Maybe I could write to him. Unfortunately my mother kept only the letters, not the envelopes with the return address. There was a mention of a post office box, but that had been set up in the early seventies. I doubted that Sam had kept it after my mother's death.

E-mail. Maybe he had an e-mail address.

By the time I had finished drying myself off, I had a plan. I went straight back to my room and switched on my computer. I knew that my mother's coven's name was Ròiseal, so I did a search. To my amazement, something popped right up. It was a Web page for a magick shop called Bell, Book, and Candle, in Salem, Massachusetts. The person who made the page listed himself as a member of Ròiseal. At the bottom was a link to contact the Web master. I clicked on it, and a blank e-mail popped up. What would I say? I had no idea who this person was or how well he or she knew my uncle. I had little to say, so I had to keep it very simple.

Dear Sir or Madam,

I'm trying to get in touch with my uncle, Sam Curtis. If he is still a member of Ròiseal, could you forward this note to him? I would really like to meet him or speak to him, but I do not have his address or phone number. This means a lot to me, so I would really appreciate the help.

Many thanks,
Alisa Soto

Turning off the computer, I had a huge sense of satisfaction, a deep feeling of release. It was really strange, since all I'd done was act on an impulse. Of course, this pleasant feeling was going to evaporate quickly if I didn't get to school in the next eighteen minutes. I pulled on my clothes and ran for the door.

2

Contact

December 17, 1944

The ghosts have been getting more and more wild. They break things regularly. Mother and Father wrote to some specialists from Boston who came last night to examine the house for signs of haunting. They did seem to detect a strange energy, but they couldn't pinpoint anything that could help us identify or deal with our poltergeist. Some experts!

When I am initiated in a few months, I will have access to the family library. Right now I don't even know where it is—it's carefully protected by layers of spells. Our store of knowledge is said to be one of the most impressive of any coven in the area. Surely we must have something there that would help guide us and solve this problem. I feel strongly that this is so . . . I can barely explain it. My anticipation grows every day.

—Aoibheann

Once Mary K. and I had settled ourselves in her bedroom after school (with a huge assortment of snacks, of course), she gave me all the latest on Mark, the current object of her affection. She'd finally worked up the courage to ask him out, and of course he had said yes. Mary K. is perky and adorable, and she drives the menfolk crazy, unlike myself. They had a date set for Friday. I listened distractedly as she ran through all the possible options for the location of the big event.

"So," she concluded, "what do you think?"

Oh, man. I hadn't been paying attention. I vaguely remembered hearing something about going to Colonel Green's, the new theme restaurant that had just opened near the mall. It was supposed to look like an old sportsmen's club, and it had a handful of little secluded tables with curtains around them, perfect for a first date.

"Dinner," I said, grabbing a handful of chips. "Good idea. Colonel Green's."

"You were completely tuned out," she said, but not angrily. "Weren't you?"

"Kind of," I admitted. I took a deep breath. "I need to talk to you about something."

"What's up?" she said, concerned.

"You asked me what's been going on recently, why I've been so distant."

"I've been worried about you," she replied, popping the top of a bottle of iced tea and setting the cap on the ground for Dagda, Morgan's kitten, to bat around.

Okay. Just come out and say it.

"I'm a witch," I blurted. "Just like Morgan."

Mary K. flinched just a bit, then seemed to try to ignore what I was saying by going through the contents of her bag. "I know you were in that thing she goes to ... that Kithic thing."

"It's more than that," I explained. "My mother was a witch. I'm a blood witch."

She looked up at me, frozen.

"What do you mean, your mother was a witch? What's a blood witch?"

"Do you remember that book Morgan had here the other week?" I asked. "The one I kept staring at? That book was my mother's Book of ... her diary."

"How could Morgan get your mother's diary?" she asked shortly. "That's ridiculous. Do you hear what you're saying?"

"I know what I'm saying," I said with a sigh, "and I know how it sounds. But it's true. My mother was a blood witch. I can ... do things. ..."

"You're trying to tell me that you have magical powers?" she said. "Is that it?"

Oh, God.

"You've been sick," she said, agitatedly shaking out the entire contents of her bag onto the floor. "You're stressed out about what's happening with your dad."

"I wish that was it," I said. "I wish I was just imagining all of this. But I'm not. This stuff is real. It's not some dumb high school trend or some kind of Ren Faire spin-off club. Witches are real. I have the book here. I'll show you."

I reached into my bag to get my mom's Book of Shadows. I always carry it with me. She held up her hand, indicating that I shouldn't bother.

"I don't understand," she said, her brown eyes blazing. "We were going to write that letter to the paper. Now you're telling me that you're back into this witch stuff, just like that, and that somehow Morgan had some book that said your mother was a witch?"

"Look, I didn't mean to upset you." I hung my head. "I would give anything for this not to be true. It's not a choice."

We were both silent for a few minutes. The only noise came from Dagda trying to chomp on the bottle cap.

"Alisa," she said sadly. "I'm sorry, but I don't know what to do with this."

"Neither do I," I replied, running my finger along the seams of her lemon-colored comforter. She took a pretzel out of the bag and dropped it to the floor. Dagda pounced on it in excitement. "I should probably go," I said quietly.

Mary K. looked unhappy, but I think we both realized that our conversation was over. There was just a lot of dead air between us, and it was making both of us uncomfortable.

"My parents aren't home yet," she said. "Neither is Morgan."

"It's nice out," I said. "I'll walk home."

We looked at each other; then she turned her attention to her books, her face drawn. I quietly let myself out.

Morgan drives the weirdest car I have ever seen in my life, some kind of monster from the early seventies. It's huge and unbearably ugly, with a white body and a blue hood, and she treats it as if it were her very own child. She was docking this scary ship in the driveway when I came out her front door. I stopped, and she stepped out of the car and looked at me.

"What's wrong, Alisa?" she said, eyeing my slumped shoulders.

"I just told Mary K. the truth," I said flatly. "That I'm a blood witch like you."

She exhaled loudly and leaned back against the car.

"How'd that go?" she asked.

"It sucked."

She frowned. At least she understood what it was like for me. I knew that when she'd told her family, it had ended up being a royal mess. Things had improved for her, though ...maybe they would for me, too.

"How about a ride home?" she asked. I nodded my thanks. She climbed back into the car, and I got in on the passenger's side.

"Mary K. will come around," she said, trying her best to cheer me up.

"No, she won't," I said, playing with the window crank. "You know that as well as I do. This isn't something that people come around to."

"Want to have an informal circle?" she asked. "It might clear your mind a bit. How about we go to Hunter's?"

Morgan's boyfriend is Hunter Niall, the leader of Kithic. Hunter had really intimidated me until very recently. He's an imposing guy—very good-looking and tall, with chiseled features and piercing green eyes. He's always, always serious. To top it all off, he's British, with this exacting accent. But I had gotten to know Hunter a bit better recently, and I'd seen that he wasn't so scary after all. Even if I'd wanted to go and have a circle with them, though, I couldn't.

"It's all right," I said wearily. "I have to pack up my room or I'll be grounded until I'm twenty."

"Pack up your room?"

I explained Hilary's master house-arranging plan, and Morgan gave me a sympathetic look.

"This hasn't been a great month for you," she said.

"For you, either."

"No," she agreed. In the process of dealing with the dark wave, Morgan had confronted her father—a very powerful, and apparently evil, witch named Ciaran. Morgan had assisted Hunter and some of the others in catching him and stripping him of his magickal powers. From what I'd heard, that had been pretty awful. "I guess not," she said with a sigh. "Maybe it's never easy to find out you're a blood witch. That's something that Hunter and the other witches can't quite understand. They don't know what it's like to have regular family members and witch blood. We're unique."

How about that? Morgan and I, two of a kind.

"So," she said, pulling up to my house, "see you on Saturday for the circle? I can pick you up at seven-thirty if you want."

"That would be great," I said. "Thanks."

I ran through the door and straight to my room, trying to avoid contact with the Hiliminator. While I didn't see the woman herself, she had left a stack of folded boxes, tape, and markers by my door as a sign of her presence. How very kind it was of my stepmonster-to-be to provide me with moving supplies. It made me feel warm all over. I pushed the pile through the door and shut it behind me.

My first thought was to check my e-mail. I expected nothing, but there was a little envelope on the corner of my screen when I logged on. I quickly opened the note. It read:

Alisa,

Sam Curtis is indeed a member of Ròiseal. I for-
warded your note on to him. He seemed very excited to
hear from you. You should be getting a response soon.
Blessed be,
Charlie Findgoll

At last, one single piece of good news.

That night I dreamed of the mermaid again. The dream
was almost identical to the one the night before. This only
increased my conviction that there was something going
on in Gloucester that I needed to find out about.

At school on Friday, Mary K. seemed standoffish, so I
ended up eating lunch alone and going home by myself.
When I got there, I found that Hilary had bought rattan
boxes for diapers, new sets of shelves, and a lamp shaped
like a baby giraffe. I noticed there was nothing new planned
for the closet down the hall—no swatches, no carpet sam-
ples, no new pieces of furniture. She had gotten me some
more folded boxes, though.

After taking these to my room, I hurried to my computer
and got online. There was another note. I saw that the
sender was Sam Curtis. I couldn't even open it for a
moment, and I just sat there, staring at the name. Then, my
hand shaking slightly, I clicked on the note.

Alisa,

I could barely believe it when Charlie sent me your
note. I usually don't like e-mail, but this was a major

exception! I am so happy to hear from you! I think about you often, and I want to know all about you.

I only have a computer at work, so here is my phone number and address. Write, call, visit . . . or all three.

—Sam

I didn't know quite how to respond. I'd acted so quickly in sending the note that I hadn't really come up with a complete plan about what to do if Sam actually wrote back. If I called him, my father would question the long-distance charge. Visiting—that sounded great, but how was I going to go to Gloucester, especially without my father knowing?

Quickly, hands shaking, I printed out the note and tucked it into my mom's book. Then I trashed the note from my in-box. I didn't want anyone finding the letter by accident when they were going online. My father didn't know anything about my mother's heritage, and Hilary certainly didn't, either. This was private, between my uncle and me.

At dinner (a pregnancy blue plate special: cold soba noodles and baked lentil burgers) Hilary actually looked worried about me when I left my plate untouched. She offered to get me whatever I wanted—pizza, burgers, anything. It was my father who said that he wasn't going to give in to my "moods." When he ordered me to stay in for the night and work on my room, I went along with it quietly. I was too preoccupied, and too afraid of being grounded, to argue.

The next morning, the beginning of spring break week, I was still fully engaged in this process. Admittedly, I spent most of my time unearthing old magazines and reading them, sorting out old piles of letters and birthday cards, sifting through clothes and shoes that I didn't wear much and moving them around. The boxes sat in the corner, still folded.

I could tell Hilary had no idea what to say to me. She was starting to lose her patience, and she made frequent passes by my door. On the one hand, every time she looked, I was working. She saw me shuffling things around. On the other hand, nothing was really being accomplished. All of my posters and pictures were still on the walls, and the contents of the drawers were spread all around. In fact, my cleaning had only resulted in a huge mess. By six o'clock that night all I had managed to do was put my socks into a laundry bag and move them to the other room. I was dressed and ready for Kithic's weekly circle a half hour early, though.

"You know," said Hilary, leaning in my door and staring at the massive pile of magazines and loose papers at the foot of my bed, "we're going to need to start moving this furniture on Monday. Things don't quite look ready."

"Oh," I said, thanking God as I heard Das Boot's engine, signifying Morgan's approach. I grabbed my purse and headed for the door. "They will be. I just had a lot of junk to go through. It will all be in boxes tomorrow. You'll see."

3

Flood

April 14, 1945

Today is my fourteenth birthday, and I will be initiated tonight. I've worked hard, and I've studied all my lessons. I know I am ready. Still, it's hard to sit and wait until evening comes. I guess I am a little more nervous than I would like to admit.

I spent the morning arranging all of my books perfectly on my shelves, but the ghosts came and pulled them all down when I stepped out of my room. They must know I am looking for a spell to make them go away. They do things to me because they know I will succeed. It makes them angry.

Tonight after the ceremony Mother has promised to show me the location of the library. Finally! Everything I've prepared for and dreamed of . . . Goddess, be with me today!

—Aoibheann

Every time I see Hunter Niall, I'm struck by his amazing good looks. There's no way not to notice them. It's like getting hit in the eye with a baseball—you just can't help but be aware of something striking like that. I was aware of them as he greeted us at the door of his house. He's really tall and very lean, all muscle. His hair is a golden blond. I don't think he goes to much trouble to get it cut well, and I'm absolutely sure he doesn't style it. It just always looks good naturally, all tousled. On top of it all, there's the sexy British thing. Enough said.

"Da's out tonight," he said, opening the rickety screen door for us. He smiled at Morgan and gave her a welcoming kiss. "He won't be back until well after the circle is over."

I flushed. Must be nice to have a love life. I assumed that Hunter noticed my reaction or read my mind because he laughed.

"My father doesn't go out much," he explained. "He's not very social, as you might have noticed. This is a big step for him. He's having dinner with Alyce Fernbrake, then they're going to do some research on medicinal uses of milk thistle."

"I didn't think anything," I said, immediately implicating myself. I backed into the hallway. "I'll, uh, go in. . . ."

Candles were burning in every corner of the living room, giving it a romantic glow. Everybody looked comfortable, but it seemed like I was surrounded by couples. There were Robbie Gurevitch and Bree Warren, Ethan Sharp and Sharon Goodfine, and Jenna Ruiz and Simon Bakehouse. Then there was Raven Meltzer, decked out in a black shirt so sheer that there was no point in wearing it. She was sitting cross-legged on the floor, examining the design on a tarot card, then looking at her arm. I had a feeling she was considering another tattoo and wondering how much biceps real estate this particular picture would take up. Raven, while she had no current significant other, was never really single. Matt Adler was sitting next to her at the moment. I knew they had fooled around at some point.

So there I was. Painfully alone Alisa. I felt like I had wandered through the wrong door, into some kind of couples' encounter session instead of the coven meeting I was supposed to be at.

"I think we have everyone for this evening," Hunter said as he and Morgan walked in side by side. "Thalia is under the weather, so there will be eleven of us."

He drew the circle in salt. We blessed the four elements—fire, earth, water, and air—and performed a power chant to bring energy to our circle. Hunter sat us all down and started the ritual for that week.

"Some of us haven't been feeling well lately," he said. I thought he must be referring to the dark wave that had almost engulfed Widow's Vale just days before. As it approached, it had made all of the blood witches incredibly sick. Morgan and Hunter had recovered. My head was still sore from where I'd hit it on a gravestone while we were in the old cemetery, fighting the dark wave. Hunter's father, Mr. Niall, was still weak.

"It's true," said Bree. "This is a really bad time for allergies and the flu."

I almost laughed, but I was able to hold it in.

"Actually," Hunter said, "the purpose of this exercise is to clear our minds of things that have been troubling us. It's designed to purge us of negative feelings that we may be holding back, feelings that may inhibit our personal progress.

Sometimes illnesses are related to emotions, and when we release some of the bad ones, we can experience improved well-being."

He had placed a little cauldron in the middle of the circle. This was full of twigs and bunches of herbs. Next to it was a small pile of handmade papers and a box of pencils.

"Clear your mind for a moment," he said, "and concentrate on finding something that's blocking you. Then I'd like everyone to take a piece of paper from the center," he went on, pointing at the papers. "Write down what you've come up with. Something that causes you pain. Be as clear and concise as possible. When you're finished, fold the paper and put it into the cauldron."

Those little papers weren't going to do the trick for me. I needed something a bit more sizable, like a three-subject notebook. Everyone else seemed fine with it, though. Raven scribbled just one word, then flicked hers into the cauldron. Other people took more time, carefully choosing a few words. I did my best to cram as much as I could onto the slip. When we had all completed this, Hunter took out his bolline and carved something into a dark blue candle, which he then turned and showed to us. There were two runes sliced into the wax.

"Yr," he said. "Death, the end. Then Dag, the dawn. Clarity. May the spark of this flame purify us and lift these weights from our souls and minds."

He touched the candle to the cauldron contents, and they sputtered into flames.

"Alisa," Hunter said, looking at me with a smile, "would you mind leading the chant? Just repeat the following as we go around: Goddess, I turn myself over to you. With this smoke, so goes my care."

I knew Hunter was making a special effort to include me in the ritual. After all, aside from him and Morgan, I was the only other blood witch present. This was something the others didn't know. We joined hands and began walking deasil, and I started the chant. My voice sounded squeaky and thin next to Hunter's, but I did my best to speak as clearly and boldly as I could.

At first all I felt was a kind of nice lightness, as if I was taking a brisk shower and washing off layers of emotional grime. I could actually see it coming from my skin, like a slight vapor. I sometimes saw things like that now—colors, auras—things that had been invisible to me before.

"Goddess, I turn myself over to you," I repeated. "With this smoke, so goes my care."

Some of the others had their eyes closed, but mine were open. I was fascinated by what I was seeing. The substance was coming from everyone now. Around some people it was a fine mist, but Morgan, Hunter, and I appeared to be smoldering. It was as if the fire was burning the emotion up just like the slip of paper and pushing the smoke through our pores.

"Goddess, I turn myself over to you. . . ."

We circled around and around, the energy mounting higher and higher. I felt a force rising up from me—something welling up, wanting to get out of me, jump out of my mouth or break out of my skin. It was such a powerful feeling that I had to push it down in order to keep speaking and moving, but my voice started to crack under the strain.

"With this smoke ... so goes my care."

I had written too much on the slip, I realized. I had brought up too much. The smoke was obscuring my vision, tightening my throat. It's not real smoke, I told myself. It's magick. Focus. You can breathe, Alisa. You can speak. But my voice was still crumbling to pieces. Control it! I thought.

I noticed that some of the others were acting a little strangely, looking all around and falling out of step. Then I suddenly realized why. It was just a little sound at first, and I'm not even sure when I became aware of it. All the pipes in the house were rumbling. The sink in the kitchen had turned itself on. The toilets began to flush themselves.

"It's all right," Hunter said. "Keep going, everyone." But he, too, looked around in surprise. His gaze fell on me. By this point I could barely speak or see. The force of the spell was dragging things up from every corner of my mind, every cell of my being, and I just had to keep shoving them down to keep going.

"Goddess, I ..." Every word was hard. "... turn my ... self ... o ... ver ..."

The hiss of water could be heard coming from every corner of the entire house. The shower had come on.

"What the hell *is* that?" said Raven, breaking the circle. Everyone stopped moving.

"Stay within the circle," Hunter said firmly. But it was no use. The others had already broken away in confusion. The sounds only got louder. Now the pipes thumped in the walls, trying to hold back the swell. Then they gave up the effort, and the running water took on a raging, fearsome quality. The faucets were no longer just running, they were gushing. Water could be heard hitting the floor of the bath-room above.

It was me, I realized through the haze. I was doing this with my telekinesis. I was wrecking this whole house, and I couldn't even stop myself. It was this emotion—this smoke coming out of me. Force it down! I told myself. Force it down! I gave up the chant and started slapping my body, as if it was covered in real fire that I could extinguish. But it did-n't work. Hunter quickly stepped over to me and put his hand to my forehead. A strange warmth came from him, which dribbled down over me. The smoke began to subside, and my mind began to clear. I could see everyone standing there, looking at me.

"What's she doing?" Raven asked, pointing at me. "Why was she hitting herself?"

"I'm fine," I lied, my voice hoarse.

"Perhaps it would be best to call it a night," Hunter said quickly. The others looked at one another and silently started reaching for their jackets. I felt my stomach sink. My only thought now was that if I had turned on the water, maybe I could turn it off. I lurched into the kitchen. Water came out of the faucet with such force that it actually bobbed up and down in waves. The stopper must have been plugging the drain in the sink because the whole thing was full and water was pouring out, covering that part of the floor. I reached for the knobs, but they were useless.

"Turn off," I said out loud, thinking that might work. It didn't. The water continued to gush, flooding the counter-tops and soaking the kitchen rug. I put my face in my hands. This was too embarrassing. I wanted to cry.

"Alisa, are you okay?"

Morgan was standing behind me.

"Fine," I said, backing away. "I'm fine. I just need to clean up this massive mess I'm making."

"What are you talking about?" she asked. "Mess *you're* making?"

"Hunter knows," I said, staggering over to open up what looked like a broom closet to look for a mop.

"Hunter knows what?"

It wasn't a broom closet I had entered; it was a pantry cupboard. Since I couldn't clean the floor with crackers and cans of soup, I shut the door and hung my head.

"About me. About my problem. I was going to get help. . . ."

"Help with what?"

"My . . ." Ugh. I was in no condition to explain. I didn't even have the energy to say the word *telekinesis*. It had too many syllables.

"Why don't you go sit down by the fireplace?" she said, taking me by the shoulders and leading me toward the door. "This is nothing. I'll get it."

I nodded and stumbled into the empty room where the circle had just been. Everybody else was gone. Suddenly feeling exhausted, I slumped down in a corner of the room between the sofa and the wall and closed my eyes. Everything in me hurt. It all passed through my mind, everything I'd written on the slip of paper, everything that had been eating at me. Hilary. My father. My mother. My insane powers. The dark wave. And now all the water flooding Hunter's house. The images just kept on coming, smacking into my mind like it was a punching bag.

Someone was approaching me. Without opening my eyes, I knew it was Hunter—it wasn't witch power: He was just one of the only two people left, and I heard Morgan moving in the kitchen. I felt him slide down and sit on the floor next to me. Whatever he had to say to me, I clearly deserved it. I was a freak. I was flooding his house. I was a danger to myself and others. I braced myself for the lecture I was sure he was about to give. He was going to kick me out of Kithic, I thought, just when I had realized that was the only place I found any peace. I pulled my knees into my chest to steady myself.

Instead of giving me the berating I was expecting, I felt Hunter put his long arm over my shoulders.

"Alisa?" he asked, trying to get me to open my eyes and look at him. I couldn't. He put his other hand on the back of my head, guiding it down so that it rested on his shoulder. I felt the whole wave of emotion coming to the surface. It was so powerful, it almost made me shake.

"Let it out," he said, his voice soft.

Much to my embarrassment, his words opened up another floodgate—this time in me. I started to sob. And just as with the plumbing, I couldn't control the flow.

In the distance, over my sobs, I heard the sound of the kitchen drain releasing and the water gurgling as it was sucked down into the pipes.

4

Uncontrollable

September 2, 1946

Goddess, merciful Goddess. What is happening in this house?

The event that started it all seems so trivial now, it nauseates me. Tioma had taken my favorite sweater, my pink angora one, from my room without asking, only to get ink on the sleeve. I found it in a ball at the back of the drawer. Furious, I went off to find her. She was in the living room, shrinking behind a book, as if she knew what was coming.

Of course, I was trying to control myself, but I was enraged. She stood up and tried to deny what she had done, which only made me angrier — so angry that I couldn't speak. Just as I turned to stalk back to my room, the heavy, glass-doored bookcase tipped over and slowly fell — right onto Tioma. I heard the glass shatter as it fell against her, knocking her to the ground and landing on her back. She made no sound. For a minute I thought she was dead — then I saw her fingers move.

Mother and Father weren't in the house, so it was up to me to help her. A spell came from the back of my mind, something I'd read in an old Book of Shadows—a spell for making things lightweight. Without another moment's thought I quickly performed it, and I was able to lift the bookcase off my sister's back. She looked broken. There was blood coming from all parts of her body where the glass had punctured her, but she was alive. I called out to all members of the coven, asking them to run and help. Then I started reciting every healing spell I had ever learned to stop the bleeding. Within minutes my parents and various members of Róiseal were running through the door. They rushed her off to the hospital.

Tíoma is still there and is still insensible, but the doctors say she will recover. Mother and Father praised me endlessly, telling me that my quick thinking and composure saved her life. But all I can think of is my rage—my stupid rage over a sweater—and the sight of the massive cabinet coming down on my sister.

Why do these ghosts want to harm us?
—Aoibheann

I don't know exactly how long we sat there like that, but it had to be a while. It seemed like every drop of water in my entire body was being sucked out through my eyes. Hunter just sat through it all, rocking me back and forth, like you do with crying children. I was a mess.

Finally my breakdown slowed, and he let go so that I could sit up and wipe off my face with my hands. I saw that I had completely soaked through the shoulder of his gray T-shirt. Very fitting. I was dousing everything else—why not Hunter, too?

"I'm sorry," I sputtered, my breath still jagged. "I'm so sorry. I did this. All this damage . . ."

"What happened?" he asked softly.

"I don't know." I sniffled.

"Could you feel anything physically?" he asked. "Could you sense anything happening?"

"You mean aside from the sound of the exploding pipes and the stampede of people out the door?" I said, much more sharply than I intended.

"Maybe some tea," he said, backing off the subject. He looked up at Morgan, who I suddenly realized was standing right by us. She handed me some Kleenex, which I desperately needed. "Morgan, would you mind?"

"I'm on it," she said, standing upright and heading for the kitchen.

"Use the blue canister," he said. "It's in the back."

I just sat for a few minutes after that, saying nothing, staring at the floor and wiping at my eyes whenever they teared up again. He set his arm back over my shoulders and let me lean against him. I finally worked up the will to say something.

"I didn't mean to. . . ." I waved my hand around, trying to indicate the flooding, my crying . . . basically everything that had happened that night.

"Do you think I haven't seen tears before?" he said softly. "And after the dark wave, do you think some water on the floor is really going to bother me?"

That did put it into perspective a bit.

"What's wrong with me, Hunter?" I said, unable to keep my voice from breaking.

Morgan returned with a tray full of steaming earthenware mugs and a small chocolate chip cake that must have been intended as an after-circle snack before I made everyone scatter. Hunter released me, and I pulled myself into one of the chairs in front of the fireplace. Morgan handed me a mug of the tea and sat down on the floor next to us. It was scalding hot to the touch, and I must have winced. She reached over and circled her hand above it, and immediately it cooled to the perfect temperature. I looked down at her in amazement.

"How did you . . . ?" Duh, I thought. This is Morgan. Cooling some tea wasn't exactly a big deal for her. "Never mind," I added. "Dumb question."

Hunter sat down across from me and leaned forward. He took a mug and then reached for my hand.

"It's a simple spell," he said. "A little transferal of energy. Just focus your energy. Tell yourself that the tea will cool. Know it."

I did my best to focus. He rotated my hand once over the cup, and I felt a little warmth, like I'd grabbed a hot potato and let it go. He took a sip of the tea.

"Very nice," he said with a smile. "Well done." Hunter doesn't smile too often, but when he does, he could melt a stone. He really could have been a model.

"Drink that," Morgan said, pointing at my cup. "Believe me, it works."

"Better than Diet Coke?" I croaked, rubbing the last of the moisture from my eyes.

"Almost," she said. Hunter rolled his eyes good-naturedly.

I tried a sip of the tea. It was sweet and tasted like a whole garden of herbs, nothing like the nasty concoctions Hilary bought at the health food store. This was powerful stuff, and I could feel it all through my body, spreading calm.

"Do you feel up to talking about it now?" Hunter asked, watching me as I drained the cup. I nodded. Morgan poured me some more from the pot and mixed in the honey.

"Right," said Hunter, his tone turning professional. "The exercise we did tonight was designed to help bring out and release negative emotions. A lot has happened to you recently, to say the least. You have a lot of new information. Morgan has told me that there have been some things going on in your family, too. All of that was shaken loose, and it seems to have triggered an attack."

"An attack?" said Morgan. Hunter turned to her.

"Alisa is telekinetic," he explained. "We said that we would look into the problem after the dark wave had been dealt with, and now we are."

"Telekinesis," Morgan repeated. "Is that what that was? I thought I felt something weird in the *tàth meànma brach*." Just before the dark wave had come, Morgan and I had joined minds in a ritual called a *tàth meànma brach* to fight it. She had seen everything inside my mind, and I had seen everything inside hers.

"No doubt you did," he agreed. "Could you get a clear idea of what was going on?"

"No," she said. "It was a strange sensation, but I didn't really know what to make of it. It felt like an electric shock, but a mental one. I thought it was coming from the dark wave."

"All that stuff that happened to you—the shelves in the library, the butter dish in the kitchen—that was all me," I said, looking down at her. I was referring to various instances of things falling over or flying around in the last few weeks. Several had ended up heading for Morgan, and she'd seemed really upset by them. "I didn't mean to do those things. In fact, at the time I didn't even know it was me."

"So the deflection spell . . ." she started to say, turning pale. "It put you in the hospital. Oh, Goddess."

I wasn't sure what she was talking about, but Hunter nodded to her. "It wasn't Ciaran at all," he said. "But to get back to the problem at hand," Hunter went on thoughtfully, "aside from helping to release your emotions, the spell obviously triggered something. It would be very hard to tell what exactly that was. It's a general release spell with a broad range. How did you feel when we were performing it?"

"It was so strong," I said, remembering it with a shiver. "These feelings . . . I felt like a volcano. I kept trying to push the emotions down. I didn't even know what was going on until I saw everyone panicking."

He drummed his fingers on his knee and looked thoughtfully into the fire for a moment.

"Judging from what I've seen so far," he said, "I'd guess the phenomenon is somehow connected to your emotional state. I remember that objects would fall when you became frustrated with learning the dark wave spell. Tonight the flooding stopped when you started to cry."

"That's it?" I said hopefully. "So how do I stop it?"

"Its exact mechanism will be bit more complicated to determine, I'm afraid," he explained. "These things are rarely easy. You may react to certain substances or elements more than others, or you might be attuned to certain magnetic or magickal forces. In order to draw up that much power, you're tapping into something fairly deep—probably a whole web of energies."

Wrong answer. He was supposed to say that this was a cake problem and that he had a book that would fix it *right here.*

"How long have you had this condition?" he asked.

"My whole life, I guess," I said, picking at the flecks of herbs that floated to the top of my cup. "Weird little things have always happened to me. I just used to think that I was very unlucky and clumsy. But it's gotten a lot worse recently. My mother had it, too. She talks about it in her Book of Shadows."

"That's very significant," Hunter said, furrowing his brow. "Very significant. I didn't know that. Is there anything else you've noticed about these episodes? Do they have anything in common? Anything at all?"

"Not really," I said. "Nothing I can think of."

Hunter got up and started to pace a bit. He seemed to be thinking the problem out. I noticed that the cuffs of his jeans were soaked, as were his boots. "I know a man in London named Ardán Rourke," he said. "This kind of thing is his specialty."

"What kind of thing?" Morgan asked. "Telekinesis?"

"Uncontrollable magick, in any form. It's too late to ring him now—it's after two o'clock in the morning there. I'll try tomorrow. There's also Jon Vorwald, a Burnhide who works out of Amsterdam. He might be able to tell if it's a magickal reaction to certain metals or other substances, which it very well might be. I'll contact him, too. In the meantime I'll talk to Bethany Malone. In fact, let's see if she's home now."

He went into the kitchen for the phone. Morgan reached up and took my hand. I felt a warm flow of energy coming from her, soothing some of my frayed nerves.

"I wish I'd known," she said.

"I just figured it out a little while ago," I said. "It was news to me, too. I never meant to do anything to you. You know that, right?"

"Of course," she said.

"No answer," Hunter said, coming back in and breaking himself off a handful of the cake.

"Do you want me to scry for her?" asked Morgan.

"No." Hunter shook his head. "I'll try again tomorrow, after I talk to Ardán and Jon."

"I need to wash my face," I said, wanting to get up and be alone for a moment. I suddenly felt like some kind of leper. All this talk of phenomena and metals and bringing in specialists from London and Amsterdam was too much. Was my problem so bad that it required a *global effort* to fix?

Hunter shifted uncomfortably. "I'd use the upstairs one. The downstairs is still . . . very damp."

In the upstairs bathroom there was a thin film of water covering the black-and-white-tiled floor. Hunter had thrown down a few towels. They were strewn around the various puddles, swollen and heavy, like enormous slugs. Water had pooled into a kind of lake under the claw-foot tub. If this was the drier of the two bathrooms, I really didn't want to know what the downstairs one looked like.

Though I had soaked the place, I could see that it was otherwise spotlessly clean, even austere. Soon it would smell like mildew, thanks to me. I picked up the towels and wrung them out as best I could into the tub, then hung them from the shower rod.

My face was also a damp wreck. My huge eyes were completely bloodshot, and the lids were puffy. I looked gross, froglike. I splashed cold water on my face until it seemed less swollen, then dried it on one of the hemp washcloths that hung from the towel bar.

When I came back into the living room, Hunter and Morgan were huddled together in discussion. They separated as I entered.

"Are you feeling any better?" Hunter asked, rising to give me his chair.

"I think I should go home," I said.

"I don't think that's advisable, Alisa," he said. "You've just been strongly affected by a spell. I think you should stay here until it wears off a bit."

"I'd really like to go," I said quietly.

Hunter studied me for a moment, and I felt a weird sensation come over me, as if someone was trying to climb inside my skin.

"What's that?" I asked.

They both raised their eyebrows.

"You felt that?" said Hunter.

"Yeah," I said, running my hands over my arms. "It was creepy. What was it?"

"That was us," he said. "We were casting our senses out to you, trying to get information about how you felt."

So they were witch-spying on me. At least he was honest.

"Have you ever felt it before?" he asked.

"No," I said. "Why? Have you done it before?"

"Very strange," Hunter said, not answering my question. He rubbed at his chin, then nodded to himself. "Right, then. I'll take you, if you really want to go. Morgan, you might want to have a look at those books on pyromancy while I'm gone."

A minute later I slid into the passenger's seat of Hunter's old Honda and stared into my lap. Seeing that I wasn't in the mood to talk much, he turned on the radio, but it didn't work very well. All he could get was a static-ridden country station. After a few minutes of trying to get something else, he grimaced and switched it off.

"Unbelievable," he commented, shaking his head. "We witches can tap into the power of the universe. We can rip holes between life and death. But we still can't get an old radio with a bent aerial to pick up anything besides crackly country and western."

I couldn't help but smile at that.

As we pulled up in front of my house, Hunter turned to look at me.

"I'll try to have some answers by the morning," he said. "For now, just get some rest."

"Okay," I said, reaching for the door release. As I was getting out, he reached up for my arm. I turned to see him stretching over the passenger's seat to look at me.

"Ring me if you have any more problems tonight," he said. "I don't care what time it is."

He waited until I was inside before pulling away. I could hear my dad and Hilary in the kitchen, talking about their plans for converting my room into the Hilspawn habitat. I took from what they were saying that they had just gone out to order a crib and a dresser. Now they were making a list of objects to put on the gift registry—the monitor, a sliding rocker, a Diaper Genie. . . .

In their excitement they didn't even notice that I had come home, which was fine with me. I headed off to my room. I wanted to enjoy it while it was still mine.

5

Explosion

October 29, 1948

A strange thing happened today. I was down in the library, looking through some old books on the elder futhark alphabet. These particular books are rarely used, so they're kept well in the back. As I pulled the book from the shelf, I noticed another book wedged behind it.

To my amazement, it turned out to be a Book of Shadows that belonged to my great-great-grandmother, Máirín Quinn. How it had gotten lost like that for so many years is beyond me. Our family has always taken great care with its books, especially the Books of Shadows. Stranger still, some of the pages have been violently torn out. It's not like a Rowanwand to mar a book in any way. I wonder what happened. I'm going to read the book tonight, then I'll make sure it's filed away in the proper place.
—Aoibheann

Even before I turned on the light to my room, I knew that something was wrong. Things were different. There should have been shoes by the door for me to trip over. Somebody had changed things in here. Had my attack done something to my room as well? I flicked on the light and discovered the worst.

My belongings were in boxes. Clothes. Shoes. Posters and pictures from my walls. One box was full of books, including my mother's Book of Shadows and mine. It took me a frantic minute even to find Sam's letters—they were packed in with a bunch of old papers from the floor. They were bundled together and retied in ribbon. I felt my stomach clench.

This had to be the work of Hilary. For her to have gone through my stuff was bad enough, but she had been handling *my mother's personal property*. Had she read the letters? My book?

My brain couldn't even put those thoughts together. Insane, raging, I blew open the door and tore through the house. This was it—I couldn't hold it back any longer. I found them still sitting in the kitchen, giggling over something.

"What's the matter, honey?" my dad asked.

I must have looked like something from an alien movie. I felt my eyes bulging and my heart racing. My hands were clenching and unclenching.

"What did you do?" I hissed.

"Oh," Hilary said, as if just remembering, "I did some cleaning in your room."

"*Cleaning?*" I spat. "You didn't clean—you went through everything I own, everything personal. . . . You went through my mother's things. . . ."

They fell silent and looked at each other.

"I didn't go through them, sweetie," she said. "I just put

them in boxes."

"First of all," I said, my energy on the rise, "I'm not your sweetie. My name is Alisa. And I'm sorry that I've been inconveniencing you with my presence, but I live here, too. You can't just wish me away. I know you're in a big rush to move me down to the storage spot at the end of the hall, but that gives you—"

"*Alisa!*" my father yelled. "Watch your mouth! I know you're upset, but Hilary's pregnant. Think of what she's going through!"

"What *Hilary's* going through?" I yelled in disbelief. "What about me? You let Hilary come in here, take over the house, order me around. You barely even know I'm alive. I have to eat her horrible food, and move all my things, and listen to her puke."

"How dare you talk about her that way!" my father said, barely able to control himself. "This is the woman who is going to be your stepmother. You have to show her respect!"

"*Please!*" I groaned. "She's practically my age! What, couldn't you find anyone *younger*? Why didn't you just ask me? I could have introduced you to some freshmen at my school."

I knew I had entered uncharted, dangerous territory, but I couldn't seem to stop myself. It was like my jaw had become unhinged or something, and every terrible thought I'd ever had was spilling out. I wondered if the spell was still affecting me, allowing me to let fly with all my thoughts and emotions. I knew I was digging myself into a very deep hole.

"You're just marrying her because you got her pregnant," I hissed, all control gone. "Because you were *stupid*. You were both stupid. And I've got to suffer because the two of you don't know how to control yourselves."

Hilary began to cry, and my father's face turned purple. He turned to me with more rage than I have ever seen him show anyone. All at once it hit me what I'd done. I'd told them everything I'd been thinking—everything I hadn't wanted to say. On top of it all, the spice rack fell off the wall.

Oh, God. Oh God oh God oh God.

Before he could even retort, I decided to get the hell out of there. I didn't ever want to know what he was going to say to that. I ran back to my room and slammed and locked the door. This was bad. This was very bad. My life was about to take an abrupt turn for the worse, if such a thing was possible.

A thought suddenly flashed into my mind. *Gloucester.* I would go to Gloucester. *Now.*

It was an insane idea, but not much more insane than the thought of going back into the kitchen after that conversation. Really, there was no better time to go. Besides, didn't my mother's family have a right to have me if my own father couldn't be bothered? Something had been telling me to go there. Now I would listen to it.

Impulsively I grabbed my duffel bag. I put in my mother's Book of Shadows, the printout of Sam's e-mail, some random clothes and things from my dresser. What else would I need? I looked around and took my warmest sweater, a hairbrush, and my own Book of Shadows and stuffed my purse right on top. That was it. The bag was full, and I felt that I needed to move quickly before my father recovered enough to come after me.

I peeked out into the hall. No one was there. I could hear

fevered talking in the kitchen. As silently as possible, I crept down the stairs. Fortunately you can't see our front door from the kitchen, so I was able to slip out. I ran, as quickly as I could, across our neighbors' yard and down the street. I knew it wouldn't be long before my dad figured out that I had given them the slip, and then he would be out on the street, looking for me.

Once I was away from the house, I realized that I didn't have a second move planned out. When I slowed down to a walk, I saw that I had been going in the direction of the Rowlandses' house. It was probably right around Morgan's curfew. She would have to pass the local playground on her way home from Hunter's. I headed for it and tucked myself in behind the spiral slide so that I wouldn't be easily seen but I would still be able to scan the road. About ten minutes later the distinctive shape of Morgan's car made its way around the corner. I came out from where I had been hiding and waved her over. She slowed, looked out the window in surprise, then came to a stop.

"Alisa," she said, "what are you doing?"

"I need help," I said, not quite sure how to explain myself. That statement seemed to cover a wide range of options. She looked at me, with new tear trails running down my face and an overnight bag in my grip.

"Get in," she said, reaching over and unlocking the door.

I got into the passenger's side. She pointed to the bag.

"What's going on? Did you just run away?"

"Something like that," I said, slouching low in the seat in case my dad passed by. "Would you mind driving around a little?" I asked sheepishly. She started down the street, torn between looking at the road and looking at me.

"Alisa," she said, her voice serious, "nothing that happened tonight was that big of a deal. You know we've been through a lot worse. And Hunter will have some information in the morning to help you."

"This isn't about what happened at the circle tonight," I said. "Not entirely."

"Fight with your parents?"

"Uh-huh."

"Was it about magick? Did you have another problem with the telekinesis?"

"No," I answered, shaking my head. "It's a lot more complicated than that."

"Do they know you're gone?"

"I don't know," I said, playing with the zipper on my bag. "Maybe. If not by now, soon."

She glanced at me. I felt my body tingle, and I guessed that she was looking me over in some magickal way, trying to figure out what I was thinking. She'd seen me flood a house and then sob on her boyfriend's shoulder for half an hour. Now she'd just found me hiding by a swing set at midnight with my clothes in a bag. The evidence would suggest that I wasn't entirely stable.

"Come on," she said, "I'm taking you back to Hunter's." She started heading for Valley Road, which led to Hunter's house. I was surprised she didn't speed me to the closest mental hospital. "I'd take you to my house," she continued, "but between my parents and Mary K., that would just cause you a whole new set of problems. You can stay with Hunter for a few hours, and then he can take you home."

"No," I said, clutching my overnight bag to my stomach.

"Please. No."

She pulled over to the side of the road and put the car into park.

"Why not?" she asked.

I shook my head, willing back the new storm of tears that was welling up inside.

"Look," she said gently, "you don't have to be embarrassed because he saw you so upset. Hunter can handle that. Trust me, I've turned to him enough times."

"I know what I have to do," I said, my voice wobbling.

"What's that?"

"I need to go to the bus station," I said. "I have to go somewhere."

"No way," Morgan replied, reaching for the shift. "It's Hunter's or it's home. Which will it be?"

"I have to go see my mother's family, Morgan."

That stopped her for a moment, so I jumped right in.

"It was instinct that made me take my mother's Book of Shadows from your house," I said, the words coming quickly now. "Then my telekinesis made my jewelry box fall over and break—that's how I found my uncle's letters. And I've been having these dreams, visions of my mother's hometown. I've been in touch with my uncle. He told me I can come anytime I want."

Morgan stared out in front of her and drummed her fingers on the steering wheel, deep in thought. Along with her witch skills, Morgan had a powerful big-sister vibe. Right now I could see the two were in conflict.

"Come on," I said, "how am I going to explain this to my father? How am I going to tell him that my mother was a witch, that she stripped herself of her powers, and that I've been having visions and problems with telekinesis? When you and I say that our parents don't understand us, we're not just angsting."

She couldn't deny anything I'd said.

"I still think we should go to Hunter's first," she said slowly. "You can talk it over with him."

"It's not that I don't want to talk to Hunter," I said, "but I need to get out of here. If I wait until morning, my dad will have the police after me."

Absolute silence for about two minutes.

"Tell me where you're going," she finally said.

"Gloucester, Massachusetts. To my uncle Sam Curtis's house."

"Do you have enough money?"

I reached into my purse and fished out my wallet. "I have my bank card and six dollars in cash."

"How much do you have in your account?"

"Just over three hundred," I said, "from babysitting."

Without another word, she put the car back into drive and turned it around, back toward the bus station. I could tell the internal battle was still raging on, though.

"I don't like it," she said, breaking the long silence, "but I guess I understand."

There were no cars in the bus station parking lot, and I saw no one through the plate-glass windows. It was empty, except for the plastic seats and a few ticket machines. Morgan hunched down to look at the place through my window, then she groaned loudly.

"I can't believe I'm letting you do this," she said, her voice low. She lifted herself from her seat, pressed her hand into the pocket of her jeans, and produced a few crumpled notes.

"Here," she said, pressing them into my hand, "take this, too. It's, um . . ." She smoothed out the bills and counted them. "Twelve bucks."

"Thanks," I said as she pressed the wrinkled money into my hand. "I'll pay you back."

Strangely, in response she reached over, pulled back my collar, and started tickling my neck. At least, that's what she appeared to be doing.

"Is this what they mean when they talk to kids about 'bad touching'?" I asked.

"Call either me or Hunter," she warned, drawing back her hand. "I'm serious. If we haven't heard from you within twenty-four hours, we're coming after you. I just put a watch sigil on you, so we'll be able to find you anywhere."

"Thanks," I repeated, somewhat uncertainly. I didn't actually know what it meant to have a watch sigil burned into your flesh. It sounded kind of ominous.

"I guess that's all I can really do." She sighed.

"You've done a lot," I said, stepping out and leaning in through the window. "Don't worry. I know what I'm doing."

"I have to get home," she said, obviously annoyed by the limitations of her curfew. "Be careful. And remember, call within twenty-four hours."

With that, she slowly pulled away. I watched Das Boot vanish into the night, and then I stepped inside the dingy, fluorescent glow of the bus station.

6

The Runaway

October 30, 1948

Máirín's book has opened up a whole new world to me.
Goddess, how was it that I never knew this horrific story?

Máirín's mother was named Oona Doyle. She and her husband
came over from Ireland in 1865 with a small group of other
witches. They built this house and started Ròiseal that year.

According to Máirín, a hideous influenza outbreak spread
through Gloucester in 1886. The whole coven worked as hard as
they could to combat the sickness. Young Máirín describes long
nights of visiting sickbeds and working on spells. In their attempts
to cure others, some of the members of the coven were infected and
weakened. The sickness claimed the lives of Máirín's father and her
two younger brothers, leaving the two women alone. Máirín was,
of course, devastated—but her mother's reaction was even worse.
She lost control of her mind. For two years Oona lived in this
condition, and Máirín watched over her at all times.

*Máirín describes a horrible night during which her mother
ran skyclad through the house, casting hexing spells in her own
blood. Two days later Oona's body washed up on the shore.
Oona, unable to overcome her sadness, must have wandered
out to the ocean and just kept going, allowing the waves to
overtake her. Máirín then describes the beginning of a long series
of hauntings that went on for years. She made several
attempts to control the phenomena.*

*The last few pages of the book are missing. What
Rowanwand destroys a book—much less a Book of Shadows?
What was written there? I need to study this book more closely.
I've told Mother what I found, and she seemed very interested.
Could it be that we have some kind of an answer to our haunting
problem at last?*

—Aoibheann

When I told Morgan that I knew what I was doing, I'd
probably been overstating my case just a little bit. I knew
that I was running away, that I was going to Gloucester,
and that I was going immediately. The details—well, I hadn't
quite worked them out.

I was the only person waiting at the bus station for the
midnight ride to New York. I used my bank card to buy a
ticket and sat down to wait. I felt like I was in a cheesy
movie of the week—teen leaves home, gets on bus to the
big city. Things like this weren't supposed to happen to me.
But this was real, and I was alone, seething, and nearly numb
with anticipation. Fortunately I'd timed it well, and I only had
to wait a few more minutes before the bus arrived.

About three hours later I saw the lights of New York in

the distance. Though I love the city, the Port Authority Bus Terminal, where we eventually stopped, is probably the last place I would normally want to be at three A.M. on a Sunday. Though it was less crowded than usual, there were still a lot of people wandering around. Many of these people had hollow gazes; several mumbled to themselves. Everyone seemed to be eyeing me—this squeaky-clean teen with her fat duffel bag.

According to the video monitor, the next bus for Boston left at four A.M., so I had an hour to kill. I used my bank card again to buy my ticket, taking care to have it out of my bag for the least amount of time possible. I also really needed to go to the bathroom, but there was no way I was venturing into one of those desolate ladies' rooms.

My adrenaline rush was fading. I was shivering. I passed a phone, and I thought about picking it up. I wasn't quite ready to call my father. Morgan? Mary K.? Too late. Their parents would freak. I could call Hunter. His dad wouldn't mind that I called so late (an advantage to letting your father live in your house and not vice versa). But I figured Hunter probably wouldn't be too happy about my running away, and I didn't really want to get a lecture.

No. I had decided to go, and now I was going to deal with it. So it was a little scary—I would be in Gloucester soon. I sat down and watched a screen with the weather forecast refresh itself about two hundred times before it was time to board the bus.

The bus to Boston was also almost empty, so I had two seats to myself, nice and close to the driver. This made me feel a little more secure. He didn't seem to notice anything strange about my being there alone. I guessed this was pretty much standard runaway procedure, something he'd seen before—something just like what my mother had done over thirty years before. Shoving my bag behind my head, I closed my eyes and fell right to sleep.

I dreamed of the mermaid again. It was night this time, and we were both on the shore. The sea was calm now. The mermaid hid herself under a green veil, and she pointed up to the moon, which was a hook hanging low over the water—a waxing moon. We sat in silence for a long time; then a wave lapped up on the sand. As it pulled away, the beach was glowing with runes and Gaelic words. All the space between us was filled up by this mysterious writing. Another wave came and washed it all away, leaving the beach bare and sandy. And when I looked up for the mermaid, she was gone. I woke up just as the bus was pulling into Boston's South Station, the biggest train and bus depot in the city.

I discovered by reading a few rainbow-colored folding transit maps and asking a few commuters that I needed to take two subway lines to get to North Station, where I would be able to get on a train to Gloucester at seven-thirty. From there, the ride to Gloucester would take about an hour. My brain was waxy and numb from too much emotion and too little sleep. The color-coded routes on the map seemed like they would be impossible to navigate. But I pulled up some hidden reserve of energy and brainpower and managed to get myself on the subway and across town. For the third time in only a few hours I was waiting on another platform. If only I had a car, I thought. Life would be a lot easier.

I thought of my bed back in Widow's Vale, all made, ready

to be climbed into and enjoyed. Of course, there was nothing else left in my room, but my bed was there. My dad was probably pacing. I was sure he'd been up all night. . . .

There was a phone behind me. Impulsively I picked it up and called the house collect. Someone snatched the phone off the hook on the first ring. It was my dad, who frantically accepted the charges.

"Hello? Alisa?"

"It's me, Dad," I replied, frightened by the urgency in his voice.

"Alisa, where are you?"

"It's okay, Dad," I said, keeping my eye on the track for any sign of the train. "I'm fine. I just need . . . some time."

"Time? What are you talking about?"

"It's just been too much for me to take in." I sighed.

"Alisa . . ." he said. He sounded confused, like he didn't know which would be more effective: being angry or pleading.

"I'm not just running off," I said. "I'm going to see Mom's family."

He had *no* idea what to say to that. I might as well have just told him that I'd hopped on a slow boat to China. My mother never talked about her family, so my dad always assumed that they must have been pretty bad to make her run away when she was eighteen. From what he'd told me, my mom wasn't exactly a rebel.

"There's a lot you don't know about them," I added. Understatement of the year. "They know I'm coming. They wanted to see me. I have to go."

"I've had enough of this, Alisa," he said, opting for the angry approach.

"I'm just telling you," I continued, "so you won't worry. I'm in safe hands, not out on the street somewhere. I'm going to a house, to stay with Mom's brother. There's no need to call the police or anything."

"Your mother didn't even have a brother!" he said, his voice breaking.

"She did," I said. "He lives in a nice place. It's fine. I'm fine. I just need to think. I promise that I'll stay there, where it's safe—just please don't call the police. I promise that I'll call."

He didn't know what to say. I heard his breath coming fast.

"Do I have a choice?" he finally said.

"Not really," I admitted.

"I love you, Alisa. You know that, don't you? I know you've been ..."

The train was coming.

"I love you, Dad." I felt myself choke up on that. "I have to go. Please don't worry about me."

I think he was calling my name again when I hung up. My hands shook, and my eyes stung. Onward, I thought. No turning back now.

I crashed again on the commuter train, with my head resting against the window. No dreams this time. I woke with a jolt and a crick in my neck as I heard the conductor announcing that we were pulling into Gloucester.

No one was around on the platform. Only a few people were out walking on the street—it was still early on an overcast Sunday morning, after all. I didn't know where I was or how to find Sam's house, so I just headed out and started walking in the direction that seemed most promising. I don't know how to describe it, but the town felt right to me. I could sense the heavy pull of the ocean. Lobster traps and fishing gear turned up everywhere—in signs and displays, on people's lawns. It seemed like a modest place, a functioning fishing town, very old and not very fancy. While I definitely wasn't giddy with delight, I felt a sense of calm after the chaotic night. Whatever it was that had been calling me—it was here.

A half hour later a lonely cab happened to go past me, and I frantically waved it down. The driver looked at me a bit hesitantly—I guess high school kids don't usually hail cabs off the street in Gloucester—then took me in. I gave him the printout of the e-mail with Sam's address on it and settled back in the seat. We wound up and down the tight streets filled with old colonial-style houses, many marked with plaques commemorating the people who had lived there hundreds of years ago. The cab slowed at a neat little cape house, tucked tightly in a row of similar houses on one of the town's center streets. We stopped, and the driver turned to me.

"It's all right," he said, eyeing me and my bag. "No charge."

"Are you sure?" I said, reaching into my pocket for my eighteen dollars. "I have money."

"Don't worry about it," he said. "I'm going off duty."

I must look lost, I thought. Or just really pathetic. Still, it was nice of the driver. I thanked him profusely and slid out of the car.

So there I was, standing on my uncle's doorstep at just before ten in the morning on a Sunday. I looked up above his door and saw a pentacle there—a little one, imprinted into a clay plate and carefully hung above the entrance. This was definitely the right place.

It should have felt very strange and very scary. My uncle and I were strangers to each other. But I knew that it was going to be all right. There was something about his relationship with my mother, the tone of his note, and my dreams that told me he would welcome me. With a deep breath, I rang the bell.

Meowing from inside. Lots of it. I tightened my grip on the handle of my bag as I heard footsteps coming toward the door.

"It's all right," a man's voice was saying. "Calm down, it's just the doorbell."

More frantic meowing.

"What, do you think it's a fish delivery for you guys?" he said. "Just calm down. Let me through."

The door opened.

The man who stood before me looked very boyish, though I knew he was in his forties. His hair was light brown, streaked through with golden blond and a few shots of gray. His blue eyes were framed by a stylish pair of wire-rimmed glasses. Obviously he had just been relaxing on a lazy Sunday morning, and he was comfortably dressed in a Boston University T-shirt and a pair of running pants.

"Sam Curtis?" I asked.

"Yes?" he said, looking at me strangely. He became very still and seemingly tense as he studied me. It was as if he had found a mysterious ticking package on his front step and was trying to figure out if it was a clock or a bomb.

"I'm Alisa," I said, "Alisa Soto. Sarah's daughter."

"Goddess!" said Sam, gripping the door frame. I could tell he wasn't sure if he should hug me or shake my hand. As a compromise, he decided to grab my shoulder.

"I can't believe it!" he almost whispered, looking me over. "Alisa!"

I nodded shyly.

"How did you get here? It's what, ten in the morning?"

"I got your note," I said quickly, evading his question, "and I thought it would be okay."

"Of course!" he said. "Of course! Let's get you inside."

7

Sam

Samhain, October 31, 1948

Máirín's Book of Shadows is missing. I was reading it all last night before going to sleep, and I left it on my desk. When I woke up, it was gone. I immediately ran to tell Mother. I was wild with excitement and fear, but she was very subdued when I told her it was missing. She told me not to worry, that there was nothing that could be done. Control, she reminded me. Witches must always be master of themselves. Only clear thought can produce strong magick.

Still, I feel as though I had the answer in my hands, only to have it snatched away! Oh, Goddess, what can I do?

—Aoibheann

Inside Sam's house, I was met by the comforting witchy smell of lingering herbs and incense, particularly sage. Everything was made of wood and brick, and there was a fireplace with a little fire to take off the morning chill. Two Siamese cats padded up to me, chattering their greetings.

"Meet Astrophe and Mandu," he said, picking up one of the cats and handing him to me. The cat purred loudly and pushed his head under my chin in affection. "That's Mandu," Sam said. "He's a baby, loves to be picked up. Astrophe will get you when you sit down. He thinks every lap is his."

"Astrophe and Mandu?" I asked as the cat gave me little kisses with his wet nose. "Are those magickal names?"

"No." Sam laughed. "Cat-astrophe. Cat-mandu."

I groaned, remembering my mom's description of her brother in her Book of Shadows. She'd said he was a real joker. Actually, she'd said he was asinine. I knew they'd played practical jokes on each other all the time.

"It's so early," he said. "When did you leave to get here?"

He cast a slightly strange look over his shoulder at me, but I kept my focus on Mandu, who was swatting at my hair.

"Sorry," I said. "I thought I'd take the earliest train. You know. Get a jump on things."

Lame. Obvious. But what was I going to say?

"Wait a minute," he said, "let me change into some proper clothes, and I'll make us some breakfast. I'll be right back. Make yourself at home."

With one cat in my arms and another wrapped around my ankles, I took a walk through Sam's living room. The wood floor was covered with a large Turkish rug colored in browns and oranges. On one side of the room there was a small altar, with some candles, seashells, fresh flowers, a cup, and a beautiful black-handled athame. He seemed to have about a million representations of the moon, in pictures, tiles, and masks.

Bookshelves took up most of the wall space. Rowanwands

are famous for collecting, and sometimes hoarding, knowledge. (I wasn't sure if I'd gotten much of that particular family trait.) Sam's collection covered an incredible array of subjects, from physics to literature to art. There were volumes on herbs, magick, Wiccan history, divination, Celtic gods and goddesses, tarot, and a hundred other witch-related subjects. Two shelves were devoted to volumes on astronomy. Three more were occupied by books on yoga, meditation, chakras, and Indian religion.

I noticed a few shelves that were devoted to the history of homosexuality and some current books on gay politics and culture. I was paused on these when I realized that Sam was back. He was casually dressed in a maroon short-sleeved shirt and tan pants.

"I have a lot of books, I know," he said. "Such a Rowanwand. This is nothing. You should see the family library. I think we have more books than the town library."

He noticed what shelf I was looking at and smiled.

"Oh," he said, nodding. "I'm gay."

I didn't know much about my uncle, so the fact that he was gay was just one item on a very long list. I liked his ease with the fact. I figured it had something to do with being Wiccan. I supposed they were a lot more open and well adjusted when it came to that subject. So I had a gay uncle. That was kind of cool.

"Okay," he said, directing me into the kitchen, "let's get some food for you. I can tell you're starved."

There's no use hiding anything from witches. They always seem to know. I set Mandu down on the ground and followed Sam into the kitchen.

"Do you drink coffee?" he asked.

I nodded. I was dying for coffee, actually. I hadn't slept much.

"How do you like it?"

"Sweet," I said, sitting down at the table. Astrophe, as promised, hopped right into my lap and curled into a ball. "And milky, please."

"Sweet and milky coffee." Sam nodded approvingly. "You are definitely my niece! We're going to get along well." He cheerfully put down two huge mugs and filled them up. Then he loaded in sugar and milk and pushed a cup in my direction. I took it, thanking him. It was incredible. Uncle Sam didn't fool around in the coffee department. This was the good stuff.

"All right," he said, opening the refrigerator. "Let's see. How about an omelet? I have some cheddar cheese and bacon. That might taste good."

He couldn't have known that I'd been living on mashed tofu and organic leeks for weeks now, could he? A bacon-and-cheese omelet sounded like heaven on a plate. I tried not to drool when I nodded my appreciation. For appetizers, he put some chocolate croissants, macaroons, orange slices, and strawberries on a plate for me to munch on as he worked. Munch I did. I could barely control myself. I noticed that he kept glancing back at me as he set some brown eggs, hickory-smoked bacon, and a big piece of cheese wrapped in paper out on the counter.

"I'm sorry that I keep staring," he finally said, whisking together the eggs. "It's just that you look so much like your mom."

This stopped me cold.

"I do?" I asked.

"It's kind of amazing," he said.

I had a few photos of my mom, and while I'd seen a little resemblance, I didn't think I really looked a lot like her. My father's family is from Buenos Aires, so I'm half Latina. Half witch, half Latina . . . half everything. My eyes are brown, and my hair is dark but streaked with a honey color. My skin has a warm, olive tone—not at all like the alabaster face that I saw in the pictures.

"Mom was very blond, right?" I said. "Kind of pale?"

"That's true," Sam admitted. "The Curtises come from England, and we all tend to be fair. Your coloring is darker, but there's so much of your mother in you. It's in your expression. Your face. Your height, the way you stand. Even your voice. You could be her twin."

"I'd like to know more about her," I said. "That's why I'm here."

He nodded, as if I'd just said something he'd expected to hear. Then he turned to the stove and poured the egg mixture into the pan where the bacon was cooking.

"I'm glad," he said. "I've wondered what your life must be like. I assume you weren't raised practicing Wicca?"

"No," I said, grabbing another strawberry. "I didn't know about any of this until a few months ago. I kind of stumbled into a coven at school. I saw people do things that I'd never known were possible. I've seen a lot, actually. Not all good."

He turned in surprise, then had to go back and do a little fancy pan-shaking. A minute later he presented me with the largest omelet ever made.

"Aren't you going to eat something?" I asked as he sat down.

"I will." He smiled. "Later. I'd rather talk now. You eat up."

I didn't need to be told twice. Between mouthfuls, I told Sam a little about Widow's Vale, Kithic, my dad and Hilary. This left the door open for him to start talking.

"About your mom," he said. "There's a lot to tell."

"I know part of the story," I said, accepting more coffee. "I have her Book of Shadows."

"How did you get that?" he asked, shocked.

"Through a friend, actually." I shrugged. "It just kind of turned up at her house. It seemed to have a pull on me. I actually stole it from her. She didn't mind after I told her why."

"It just turned up at your friend's house?" I nodded. Sam looked at me for a second, then laughed and shook his head. "Well, the Goddess certainly does work in mysterious ways. So you must know that your mother stripped herself of her powers. Do you know why?"

"I know about the storm," I said, feeling that was what he was getting at.

When he was young, Sam had used a book of dark magick to try to bring a little much-needed rain to the town. Instead, he accidentally produced a storm that raged out of control and killed several sailors. This was one of the events that had caused my mother to give up her magick, but not the only one. She had been pushed to the brink by her own telekinesis, which had frightened her as much as mine frightened me. The final thing that caused her to strip herself was a telekinetic incident after she argued with Sam. A table lurched away from a wall and pushed him down the stairs, nearly killing him. Sam didn't know anything about my mom's telekinesis. I could see that he thought she'd left because of his actions, and it was clear that the guilt had never left him.

"I was a really stupid kid," he said. "Beyond stupid. I had good intentions, but I produced really bad results. Horrific results."

"It wasn't just that," I said, trying to make him feel better. "She was afraid in general. She thought that her own powers were dangerous. She—"

I cut myself off. Did I want to get into the whole story of her telekinesis and mine? I would eventually, but maybe not at this very moment.

"It was a lot of things," I said. "She wrote about it. It wasn't just the storm, honestly."

He looked up, and his eyes had a glint of hope in them. He'd obviously been carrying a very heavy weight around with him for years. I felt for him.

"You know," he said, nervously shifting his coffee cup, "we know Sarah—your mom—is gone. We could sense that much—but we really don't know...."

"She died in 1991," I explained, "right before I turned four. She had breast cancer."

"Breast cancer," he repeated, taking it in. Maybe to witches that seems really mundane. For all I know, we can cure that with magick. That thought made me a bit sick to my stomach—maybe my mother could have lived....

But I was jumping to conclusions.

"Was she ill for very long?" he asked quietly.

"No," I said. "My dad told me that by the time they found

it, it was too late. She only lived for about another two months."

Sam looked stunned, shaky. For me this was old news—horrible, but something I had long accepted. He took off his glasses and rubbed at his brow.

"I'm so sorry, Alisa," he said. "I didn't know. If I had, I would have come there. I promise you."

"You didn't know," I said. "It's not your fault."

"I kept in touch with Sarah for the first few years," he explained. "But I had mixed feelings. I didn't understand why she had done the things she did. And then I went to college, got my first boyfriend—I got caught up in my life and my own dramas with our parents. I let things slide, and years went by. Pretty soon I didn't have her address, and she didn't have mine."

He saw my coffee cup was empty, and he jumped up to the stove for the pot, as if keeping me well fed and full of java helped to ease his guilt.

"So, how many people are in the family?" I asked, changing the subject. "I mean, who lives here, in Gloucester?"

"Let's see," said Sam. "There's my mother, your grandmother. Her name is Evelyn. My father died a number of years ago, as did my mother's sister. But there's Ruth, her daughter. And Ruth has a daughter your age, named Brigid. Plus there's the coven—Ròiseal. We're all family, even though we're not related. There are eight of us in all. My mother is the leader."

"Can I meet her—I mean, my grandmother?" I asked eagerly. My mother's mother. I could barely imagine it.

Sam seemed to pull back a little, though he continued to

smile. "Of course," he said, "I can take you over there as soon as you're done eating."

I shoveled in my breakfast, wanting to finish it as quickly as possible. Sam looked genuinely pleased at how much I enjoyed his cooking.

"I'll get the dishes," he said. "If you want to freshen up, there's a bathroom right by the stairs."

"That would be good," I said, wondering what I must look like after the crying jags of last night and all the lost sleep. Surprisingly, the damage wasn't too bad. I brushed my teeth and fixed my hair, pulling a thick strand of it back away from my face and off to the side, securing it with a clip I found in the pocket of my bag. Ten minutes later we were in Sam's ancient Dodge, driving up the avenue that ran along the water. We veered off, up a slight incline, into an area of dense trees. Then the trees thinned out, and I could see that we were on a high road above a rocky beach.

"This is it," Sam said, pulling over.

The house was large and imposing. It faced the water and was painted soft gray with black shutters. I saw the widow's walk my mother had written about so many times and the front porch with at least half a dozen stone steps leading up to it. There was the porch swing that she used to sit on and look out over the water. A row of thick trees and bushes bordered the property, and other tall trees dotted the front yard and lined the walk, making a shady grove.

Two cars were already parked in the driveway, so we had to park on the street. Sam unclicked his seat belt but waited a moment before getting out of the car.

"Listen," he said, "my mother is a little touchy about the

subject of Sarah. She didn't take the whole thing well. She hasn't really talked about Sarah since she left. Mother has also been under a lot of stress recently. We've had a lot going on here. So she might need a minute to get over the shock."

"Don't worry," I said. "It will be fine. I can't wait to meet her."

Sam nodded, but his brow remained furrowed. As I stepped out of the car, I felt the strong, clean breezes coming up off the water, and in the distance I could see fishing boats heading out from the harbor. It was a beautiful sight. My mother must have loved growing up here.

A splintering noise drew my attention. Sam had stepped ahead to pick up a rolled newspaper from the walk to take inside. A branch from the tree right above his head had split off and was falling—and it was huge, big enough to cause serious harm. I screamed. Sam straightened, glanced up, and jumped aside. The massive piece of wood made a sickening smack on the stone walkway and cracked in two.

"Goddess," he said, his voice full of awe. He looked from the branch to the tree, then reached down and picked up one of the broken pieces of wood.

"Are you all right?" I asked, rushing to him.

"Fine," he said, examining the branch closely. "But it's a good thing you yelled."

With one last wide-eyed look at the tree, he took me by the shoulders and hurried me to the front door. Branches fall out of trees all the time, I thought. Then again, it seemed like less of a coincidence when you considered a telekinetic girl was passing by when it happened.

Had I just done that? Had I almost killed Sam?

8

Homecoming

August 15, 1950

I've been spending more and more time with Hugh recently. He's a good man, very suitable, from a coven in Boston called Salldair. Although he is ten years older than I am, we do seem to make a fine match.

Hugh is a professor of Germanic languages at Simmons College in Boston, and he's written several textbooks. This makes him, more or less, an ideal Rowanwand husband. I know that's what Mother and Father are thinking, at any rate. They're very fond of him.

I don't really feel ready for marriage, but I know I must marry. I did fight when they first suggested it, but now I see that I was selfish and foolish. I am nineteen years old. I must accept my responsibilities. Of course, it's unthinkable that I should leave Gloucester. Our family is the head of Róiseal. As the oldest child, I will take over the coven when Mother and Father are gone. That's the way it has always been done.

—Aoibheann

Unlike my friendly reception at Sam's door, my entrance into the Curtis house was spooky from the get-go. The woman who answered the door bore only a passing resemblance to Sam. She was about the same age, and her short hair was completely blond. She seemed taken aback by my presence, as if I was standing there naked.

"This is Sarah's daughter, Alisa," Sam said quietly, forgetting any greetings.

"Goddess," she whispered, drawing back, "it's like looking at a ghost."

"This is Ruth," Sam explained to me, indicating the stricken-looking woman. "Ruth and I are cousins."

Ruth regained her composure, but her stare was still a little buggy.

"Nice to meet you, Alisa," she said.

"Is my mother home?" Sam asked, showing me inside.

"In the study . . ." Ruth replied. Her eyes were full of silent questions. Sam nodded, as if to say that he would explain as soon as he could.

Inside the house, everything was alarmingly clean. The dark, heavy wood furniture glistened. The wood floors glowed. There was nothing out of place—no piles of magazines, nothing on the steps, no stacks of mail. Just cool breezes skimming along the austere hallway, looking fruitlessly for some dust bunnies to blow around.

Sam indicated that I should wait for a moment, and then he took Ruth by the elbow and ushered her back into what looked like a colonial kitchen. I saw a brick fireplace there, along with a large wooden worktable. I could hear them talking in low, urgent voices. When they returned, Ruth looked even jumpier than before. With a final look at Sam, she knocked on the wall. I thought this was really weird, but then she reached out and grabbed two little notches in the old paneling. These turned out to be handles to a pair of ancient sliding wooden parlor doors. In opening them, Ruth revealed another room, this one small and intimate, packed closely with antique furniture. She ushered me inside.

There was an older woman working at a large desk. Even though it was a Sunday morning, she was perfectly dressed in a crisp blue blouse and black pants. Her hair was steel gray with a heavy streak of white at the front. It was cut to just above the shoulder and feathered elegantly away from her face. She had silver rings on four of her long fingers. She tapped one of these on the desk as she worked.

"Sam," she said, without looking up, "I need you to ..."

She stopped, and I saw her become aware of my presence. It hit her physically, as if her chair had shifted slightly under her, causing her to jolt. She looked straight up at me. Her pale eyes were narrow. She didn't look a lot older than my dad, but I knew she had to be about seventy. This was Evelyn Curtis, my grandmother.

A cordless phone fell from one of the tables, causing everyone but Evelyn to jump. Sam reached for it and put it back in its cradle. She seemed totally unaware of its falling. She was aware only of me now.

"Sarah?" she said, color draining from her face.

"No, Aunt Evelyn," Ruth said softly. "This is Sarah's daughter, Alisa."

Either they owned the loudest clock in the world, or it got really quiet in the study. All I heard was the ticking. This, I thought, is my grandmother. Grandmothers are supposed to want to see you all the time, to run and hug you, to give you presents. Mine scrutinized me, taking me in, head to foot.

"I see," she finally said, her eyes squinting at the corners. "Perhaps you should sit down. Ruth, could you bring in some tea?"

Ruth vanished back the way we had come. Evelyn peered at me.

"How did you get here?" she asked. "Are you with your father?"

"No," I explained, feeling my skin grow cold all over. "I came on my own. I wanted to meet my mother's—my —family."

She gave Sam a meaningful, and not entirely friendly, look.

"Alisa contacted me a few days ago," Sam said, reaching over and taking my hand. "She took it upon herself to find me. She wants to learn about us."

Evelyn stiffened and drew herself up even straighter. I was quickly grasping what Sam had been saying to me out in the car and realizing that I wasn't nearly as prepared for this as I'd thought I was. Sam gave my hand a squeeze, as if he could feel my confidence dropping.

"I see," Evelyn said again. "Perhaps we could talk for just a moment, Sam."

Sam shifted his jaw, but he nodded.

"We'll just be a minute," he said, turning to me. "Why don't you go have a look at your mother's old room?"

"Sure." I nodded dumbly.

"Turn right at the top of the stairs," he said. "It's at the end of the hall."

I excused myself and slid the study doors behind me. As I

walked up the steps, strange feelings started to flow through me—broken, choppy signals, pieces of emotions—leaving me a quivering mess. My mother's house. Here it was, just like she'd described it. The four-paneled doors with the old sliding bolts. The stairs that Sam had tumbled down. I even bent down and saw the thick chip that she had taken out of one of the banisters while she was carrying her bicycle down after Sam had stashed it on the widow's walk. It had been painted over, but the mark was still there.

This was my mother's home.

I found the room at the end of the hall and cautiously opened the door. In my imagination, I was about to be swept back to the early 1970s. My mother had described her bedroom in her Book of Shadows. The walls were blue, and she had painted yellow stars on them. There was a braided carpet on the hardwood floor. She had bamboo blinds on the windows and paper lantern lights. Her bed was covered in an old family crazy quilt. She had a portable record player and a desk with a typewriter. There were pictures of her favorite rock stars on her closet doors.

The room I found myself in was narrow and sterile, painted a plain off-white, all traces of my mother's handiwork gone. The floor was covered in a plush coffee-colored carpet. There were a neat worktable by the window, a bookcase, and a large cabinet filled with various Wiccan and household supplies. None of the furniture my mother had described remained—not even the old bed. Nothing. It was all gone, all traces of my mother ripped away. I couldn't help but think of what was still going on at my own house, with Hilary and her plans for total home domination.

For the first time on this insane trip, the weight of it all hit me. I was lost. It seemed as if my grandmother wasn't exactly overjoyed to see me. And something just didn't feel right. Everybody was on edge. I had thought that I would find my mother here somehow, or at least some loving relatives or warm memories. But this sterile room made it obvious that there was nothing here for me.

Voices. I looked around. I could hear voices. Was I going crazy now? No, I realized. There was a heat vent in the corner. I was hearing the conversation coming up from below.

" . . . and it just came down?" Ruth was asking.

"Right down. No warning . . . well, except for Alisa. It's a good thing she was there."

"How big was it?"

"Big enough," Sam said. "It would have knocked me out or worse."

"Aunt Evelyn," Ruth said, her voice full of fear, "we can't let this go on. It's worse each time. Remember what happened with Brigid and the oven. And now this. They both could have been killed."

What was this? What were they talking about? This was more than just the branch.

"The council," Sam added, his voice firm. "Mom, it's time we called them. This is really a matter for them. They have the resources, and they have specialists—"

"I have worked with specialists," Evelyn cut in. "They did nothing. I am dealing with this. . . ."

The sound of breaking glass caused me to jump, and I turned to see what had formerly been a lamp. Now it was a pile of glass pieces sitting under a cockeyed shade on the floor. I rushed to pick them up. Oh, God. Another telekinetic hiccup. The lamp was clearly unfixable. I was so desperate that I tried to spell it back together, but the truth was, I didn't know many spells and certainly not any for lamp repair. There was nothing I could do. The branch, the phone —now I'd gone and broken my grandmother's lamp.

As I fought off tears, a blond girl around my age peeked in the doorway. She had some of Evelyn's regal bearing, but her eyes were more soulful, like Sam's. Her golden hair was coiled on top of her head.

"Who are you?" she asked, looking at me as I stood there, caught red-handed with the lamp fragments. I quickly set them on the nearby bookcase.

"I'm Alisa," I said, wiping my eyes. "Sarah Curtis's daughter."

The girl looked confused, then amazed.

"I know who Sarah is," she said. "She had a daughter?"

I nodded. There I was. Proof.

"Goddess," she said brightly. "That means we're cousins, sort of. I'm Brigid. Ruth is my mom. Aunt Evelyn is my great-aunt." She stopped and cocked her head. "Are you all right?"

I wasn't sure what she was talking about for a second, then I realized that my eyes were probably still a bit teary. And there was the lamp, of course.

"Oh." I stepped away from the broken bits of green glass. "Sorry about the lamp. I, uh . . . I'm fine. I was just looking at my mother's bedroom, but I'm done now."

"This was your mom's bedroom?" Brigid said, looking around. "I didn't know that. I thought it had always been a workroom."

Brigid, at least, seemed kind of interested in me—this strange new cousin who'd shown up out of the blue, busted a few things, and seemed to know the history of her house. I guessed I'd be curious about someone like me, too.

"Are you staying here?" she asked, shifting a stack of beaded bracelets up and down her arm.

"No," I said, "I'm staying with Sam. We just came over to say hi. I don't know what we're doing now. Sam is busy talking to ... my grandmother."

"Big conference talk, huh?" she said with a smile. "Aunt Evelyn can be kind of intense. It takes a while to get to know her. You look a little freaked out."

I laughed nervously, incredibly thankful that someone seemed to understand something about my situation. "I am," I admitted. "Just a little."

"I'm about to go out," she said. "I'm going to meet my boyfriend, Charlie, for lunch. You're more than welcome to come with me. I promise I'm not as scary."

Charlie, I thought. That must be the guy from the e-mail.

"Is that Charlie Findgoll?" I asked. "I found the Web site for his shop. I wrote to him. That's how I got in touch with my uncle."

"Oh, right." She nodded. "He told me about that. You made his day. He's always complaining that no one looks at his Web site. You should come with me and meet him."

That really sounded good. Anything to get out of here.

Brigid escorted me back downstairs and boldly slid open the parlor doors. Evelyn, Sam, and Ruth were huddled together by the desk. They stopped talking the moment we walked in, which made me queasy.

"I'm going to go meet Charlie," Brigid said, unaffected by the oppressive air in the room. "I thought I'd take Alisa. You guys look busy."

"Great," Sam said, seeming very distracted. "That seems like a good idea."

Much as I wanted to avoid the topic, I had to tell them about the lamp.

"I kind of . . . broke a lamp. I don't know how. It fell off the shelf."

Ruth and Sam exchanged looks.

"What? That old green one?" Sam said. "It's fine. Don't worry about it."

Evelyn was twisting her lips into a thoughtful grimace and rearranging the alignment of her desk blotter.

"You're welcome to join us for dinner, Alisa," she said crisply. "If you would like to come back."

If this had been a movie, thunder would have cracked overhead and a horse would have whinnied. I'd never heard such an ominous invitation in my life.

"Thank you," I said, my voice a near whisper.

"We'll call," Brigid said cheerfully, leading me out.

"Six o'clock!" Ruth called to us.

That meant I would have to have to go back—unless, of course, I was prepared to run away for the second time in twenty-four hours.

9

Attraction

March 21, 1951

Mother and I have been hard at work on my wedding robe all day, and my fingers are so sore from the sewing that I can hardly hold this pen. The robe will be the most beautiful garment ever created when it is complete! We're making it from the most delicate white linen. The hard part, of course, is all of the embroidery—we're stitching in runes and symbols in oyster-colored thread, spelling each stitch. It is this work that has given me the sore fingers. And this won't be the last time. It will take us until June to finish.

Hugh has settled on getting a house here in Gloucester. He loves it here, and it's close enough to Boston. He's also decided to take time away from his teaching to write another book. Naturally I'm pleased that all is going so well. I have been a bit concerned about other things recently—Father has been looking ill. Good to know that our wedding plans are coming together without incident.

—Aoibheann

"Don't worry about the lamp," Brigid said, backing her little Toyota out onto the street. "That was just the ghost."

"Ghost?" I said. She was kidding, right?

"We have a poltergeist problem," she said, as if she was casually telling me that the house was full of termites. "Always have—it's just been getting worse recently. That's why everyone is so tense."

That did explain Sam's reaction to the branch. He had seemed concerned, more than he should have been by just a freak accident. At least he didn't suspect me, his creepy telekinetic niece who had just popped up out of nowhere—he just thought it was the house ghost. Of course. Nothing weird about that.

"It's a long story," Brigid went on. "We'll explain over lunch."

"Right," I said, eyeing a church as we passed. Poltergeists and witches, dark waves and telekinesis. What the hell was happening to me? What had I gotten myself into?

At that moment I noticed I was in a very speedy car. Brigid drove through the streets at Mach 3, squealing around corners as she felt around the console, looking for something. I gripped the seat.

"Sarah's daughter," Brigid remarked with a shake of her head. "Who knew?" She successfully came up with a CD, which she slipped into the stereo.

"You know about my mom?" I asked.

Brigid nodded. "No one talks about her, really, but everyone *knows*."

Her tone told me everything. My mother was the scandal of the century. The unmentionable. The dark blot on the family name.

At the rate Brigid was going, it took only about two minutes to drive to the town center. She pulled into a small seafood place called Take a Chowda.

"It looks cheesy," she said with a smile, "but it's good. We'll have lunch, then I'll show you around the town."

"Perfect," I said, getting out. "That sounds great."

Once inside, we seated ourselves. The place was an old diner, full of booths with Formica tables. We started looking over the menu, which consisted mainly (as I might have guessed) of different kinds of chowder, served in all different sizes and manners. If you weren't a chowder fan, this would have been a bad place to come. Brigid recommended that I get something called chowda 'n' cheddar, which came in a bread bowl.

Over the top of the menu, I saw the door open. A guy came into the restaurant and scanned the people at the tables. He was tall, even taller than Hunter, which was why I could see him. I lowered the menu to get a better look. His hair was a dark reddish brown with finger-length curled strands. He wore a pair of corduroys, a gray T-shirt with a pentagram design, and some kind of vintage tweed jacket. What really caught my attention, though, was his face. It was so expressive, with a full mouth and deep laugh lines that blossomed as he smiled. Something shot through me as he entered. It was an emotion, but it had an electric charge. There was something I immediately liked about him.

He was also just a little clumsy. As he passed through the door, he managed to get his jacket caught, which caused him to trip as he approached us. As he steadied himself, he caught my eye and smiled. I was amazed as he continued right toward us. I could see now that he had light freckles high on his cheeks and over his nose, and small peaks in his eyebrows. When he sat down with us, I knew it could mean only one thing—he was Charlie, Brigid's boyfriend. He gave Brigid a light kiss. I tried to convince myself that I wasn't disappointed.

"This is Alisa," Brigid said, pointing at me.

"Hi," he said, confirming my suspicions, "I'm Charlie."

"I wrote you the e-mail," I said quietly. "The one to Sam Curtis."

"That was you?" he asked brightly in recognition. "I was so excited! No one ever looks at my site."

"Here we go," said Brigid, rolling her eyes. "Charlie's obsessed with his site."

"Just trying to get some more business for the shop," he said with a grin. "That's why my boss loves me."

"And how many people have looked at it?" Brigid asked, egging him on.

"Seven," he said, "but I'm waiting for the big rush. It's coming any day now."

Even as he was speaking, Charlie looked me over, as if fascinated. While it would have been nice if he was doing so because he had fallen instantaneously in love with me, I knew the real reason: I give off a weird half-witch vibe. It must be like some high pitch that only full witches can hear. Brigid, though, didn't seem to notice anything odd about me, which was kind of strange in itself.

I'm so terrible at small talk. I searched my mind for something else to say. "Do you guys, um, go to the same school?"

"Charlie doesn't have to go to school anymore," Brigid chimed in. "He finished after the fall semester. He'd taken the highest levels of everything. There was nothing left for him to do."

She folded her arms and looked at him with pride, as if he was her blue-ribbon-winning entry in the state fair. He looked embarrassed.

"I'm taking some classes at the community college," he explained. "It's not like I'm just free to do what I want. But my schedule is a bit more open. I have a job at Bell, Book, and Candle in the hours between class times. It works out pretty well. I might even be able to transfer some credits when I start college in the fall."

"Wow," I said, impressed.

"It's just that, you know, we're Rowanwand." He shrugged. "Academics is what we do best."

"Speak for yourself," said Brigid, flagging down the waitress.

"So," he said, changing the subject. "You're Sam's niece? You got up here quickly. You just sent that note."

"Right . . ." I said. "You know, why wait?"

Fortunately the waitress came at that moment, preventing me from having to explain any further. Brigid and I ordered up our chowda 'n' cheddars. Charlie ordered something called a superchowda power hour.

"Sam and Alisa had an Oona moment when they came up to the house," Brigid said. "A branch almost fell on Sam's head."

Charlie turned to me in concern. "Is he all right?" he asked.

"He's okay." I nodded. "But what's an Oona moment?"

"I guess you wouldn't know about Oona," he said. "Have you explained, Brig?"

"I'd just started," said Brigid. "I didn't get that far. You can explain."

"Oona," Charlie said, slipping off his jacket, "is a relative of yours. I guess she would be your G5 grandmother."

"G5?"

"Great-great-great-great-grandmother. That's her relationship to Brigid, so it would be the same to you. It's her ghost that they're talking about."

Ghosts. Uh-huh. What next? Did they have vampires in the cellar? Unicorns in the yard?

"You're telling me that ghosts are real?" I said incredulously. "I'm still getting used to the witches."

"She's an energy," he explained, popping the wrapper off a straw. "A force. She's been around for years, causing all kinds of little problems. She used to swat things off tables, break an occasional window, rip the curtains. That sort of thing. Now objects aren't just moving or breaking—they seem to be attacking people."

"Attacking people?" Huh. The good part of this story was that it didn't sound like I was the one responsible for what had happened to Sam. At least, I didn't think so. The bad part was that I seemed to be walking into another in a series of scary situations. The fun never stopped.

"The story goes like this," he explained. "Oona's husband, your G5 grandfather, and their two sons died in a flu epidemic in the mid- to late 1800s. Oona lost her mind. It's bad when anyone loses his or her mind, but when it happens to a witch, it's really bad. If the person can't be healed, the person's coven will perform a reining spell to protect everyone, including the afflicted. In really bad cases, the person will be stripped of power. That's a horrible process. Máirín, her daughter, must not have been able to stand the thought of her mother going through it, so she tried to keep the illness hidden. It was a huge mistake. Oona ended up committing suicide."

"Oh my God," I said.

"No one knows what spells Oona cast after she lost her mind," he continued, "but it seems that one of them must have ended up lodging her energy in the house. Máirín describes all kinds of problems that started the minute Oona died."

"How do you know all of this?" I asked, feeling the hairs on my neck starting to rise.

"Aunt Evelyn found Máirín's Book of Shadows years ago," said Brigid. "But it disappeared from her room a day later. Maybe Oona took it."

"From what Evelyn's said," Charlie chimed in, "there were problems when Evelyn was a child. Then they quieted down for years and started again . . . in the, um, early seventies. After the other family problems."

He was saying that they had started around the time my mother left home. During the awkward pause that followed, the waitress brought our food. I had to admit that though the menu was a bit much, the chowder was amazing.

"What happened after my mother left?" I asked, taking a big spoonful and nodding for Charlie to continue.

"It was bad at first, I think," Charlie answered, reaching for the bowl of crackers. "I think there was a small fire and definitely some broken windows. Then the problem quieted down again. I think it only popped up occasionally during the late seventies and eighties. But in the last few months it's gone off the charts. One of the walls developed a crack. Some banisters tumbled down from the widow's walk. Two weeks ago the gas line to the oven was punctured when Brigid was alone in the house. It could have been really serious, but fortunately she smelled the gas and got out."

"We've done just about every kind of spell we can think of," Brigid added. "Now Mom's even trying to talk Aunt Evelyn into selling the house. But Aunt Evelyn won't do that. We've owned the house for over a hundred years, and she's way too stubborn to give up trying to solve the problem. She's sure that with our combined powers, we can do it. Oh, but . . ." She looked at me with what I thought was slightly exaggerated pity. "You wouldn't know anything about that. You don't have any powers."

It wasn't a bad assumption since I *shouldn't* have had any powers. It just turned out that I did. I could have told her, but somehow, "I just squashed a dark wave" wasn't going to slide right into the conversation.

"It must be *terrible* for you," Brigid went on. "How long have you known that your mom was a witch?"

"Just a couple of weeks," I said, dragging into my chowder. "I joined a coven, and then I found out later. It was a surprise."

"Well," she said, "I think it's great that you've decided to join a coven. I mean, considering that you can't do what we can do. But even though you're not a real witch, you can definitely be a part of Wicca. It's open to everyone."

Charlie started rocking his spoon on the table and stared at the wall next to us. I don't think he liked the patronizing tone that Brigid was using but didn't really want to intervene.

"I'll show you something, Alisa," she said. "Want to see me work with the rhythm of the waves?"

"Brig," Charlie said, his eyebrows shooting up, "are you, um ...?"

"Don't worry," she said. "This is a new spell I've worked out. Sending the energy out to the water. It's a really mild version of a return-to-me spell. I'd just like to show Alisa some magick. She's probably never seen any."

Since I'd just been through enough terrifying magickal phenomena to last a lifetime, it was all I could do not to laugh out loud. And considering that my uncle had accidentally killed several people while trying to help with the rain, this seemed like the worst kind of arrogant, foolish magick in the world. A party trick using the ocean? I wasn't a trained witch, but I had enough sense to know that this was a bad, bad idea.

Charlie blanched. Apparently he didn't think much of this idea, either.

Hunter had taught me a few basic deflections while I was learning the dark wave spell. I tried to find them in the back of my memory, where they were stuck together. *Nal nithrac, tar ais di cair na, clab saoil* ... which were the right words? It was as if I was grabbing at hundreds of jars of exotic unmarked spices, each tantalizing and overwhelmingly pungent, and trying to figure out how best to combine them.

Suddenly I heard Morgan's voice somewhere in my mind, just as I had when we'd joined our minds, giving me words to a spell I'd never heard before. They ran through my head, like an old song: *Sguir bhur ire, cunnartach sgeò, car fàilidh, agus eirmis tèarainte sgot.* I had no idea what the words meant, but

I understood how they worked. I was to look for a safe place to redirect the energy that Brigid was sending to the waves. I happened to be looking at the salt, so I put it there.

The saltshaker began to bounce. Brigid, who had been focusing on the waves lapping at the seawall outside the window, looked down at the noise. The shaker wobbled down the table and hit the floor. From there it rolled unsteadily to the wall near the window and stopped, unable to go any farther.

When I looked up, Charlie's amber eyes met mine and didn't flinch. His expression was unreadable, not unfriendly, but definitely serious. I felt a wave of electricity ripple through me, giving me goose pimples. He had power, lots of it, and he was sending some of it my way, casting out his senses like Morgan and Hunter had. I suddenly felt very self-conscious.

Within a second the event had passed. Brigid was flushed with embarrassment.

"Well, that didn't work right," she said.

"It was fine," Charlie said graciously. "The salt was trying to reconnect with the seawater—it was affected because it was lighter and closer to you. Working with the ocean is tricky."

"It was good." I nodded in agreement. "It was cool." Anything to make her stop.

Brigid started moving everything on her place mat around, seeming uncomfortable. Conveniently her cell phone rang. I wondered if she'd managed to spell it, too.

"Damn," she said, hanging up after a quick conversation. "That was Karen, my boss. She needs me at the shop. Sorry,

Alisa. I guess I can't show you around after all. Can you do it, Charlie?"

"Sure." He smiled at me. "I'm off today."

"Good," Brigid said, stuffing her phone back into her purse. "Alisa's coming back for dinner, six o'clock."

"Is this okay with you?" he asked, pulling out his keys.

"Sure," I said, hoping I didn't sound too eager. "Let's go."

10

Charlie

June 23, 1951

I woke up this morning to the sound of a great tearing.

When I opened my eyes, I saw that Oona had torn the front of my bridal robe—right from the collar down to within six inches of the bottom hem. My beautiful robe!

I couldn't help myself. I started weeping uncontrollably. Mother ran upstairs and came right into my room. I felt so hopeless, but she knew just what to do. She sewed up the great, jagged rip with a basting stitch. It looked like a frankenstein robe, with ugly scars. Then she put me in a hot bath filled with rosemary and lavender and instructed me to stay there for one hour, repeating the wedding day blessing. When I emerged and returned to my room, the gown was as good as new. In fact, it looked more beautiful than before. Mother had cast a glamor that concealed the tear. I am ready now, and we will be leaving soon. There is no more time for me to write.

—Aoibheann

I instantly figured out which car was Charlie's. It was a small green Volkswagen, obviously a few years old. There was a neat line of stickers on the back for different Irish and Celtic bands, including the Fianna. The thing that really gave it away, though, was the one that read, 2 + 2 = 5 . . . for Extremely Large Values of 2. I just knew that was his. Don't ask me why.

We drove around the harbor, looking at the fishing boats and the activity on the docks. He told me all about Ròiseal, how they worked a lot with the energy of the sea, and how they often had circles on the beach in the moonlight. He also explained how the coven was set up and how they worked. Because they were all experienced blood witches, they did a lot more complicated things than we did at Kithic circles. I began to wonder if Hunter found it frustrating to work with us. In comparison, running Kithic must be like watching over a bunch of kindergarteners, trying to make sure they don't eat the crayons.

"We each have a general background in magick," Charlie explained, "and we each have an area of expertise to help balance out the coven. We're all lifelong students, of course, because we're Rowanwand. This way we split up the burden of studying. Ruth does a lot of healing work. Brigid is being trained to do the same. Evelyn works in divination. Kate and James work with defensive and deflective magick."

"What about you?"

"Spellcraft," he said. "How they're written, how they're broken, how they're restricted. My dad works in the same area but on a less practical level than I do. I usually work with everyday magick. He works with the mathematical stuff relating to astronomy, sigil drawing, the Key of Solomon, things like that—right into the realm of abstract math, where numbers turn into sounds and colors and shapes . . . really hard stuff, and he also studies some very dark stuff for reference. Academic magick."

He parked the car, and we walked down Western Avenue, along the water, then up into the shopping area. As we walked, I saw that I was passing by many of the places my mother had described in her Book of Shadows. There was the chocolate shop, where she used to get chocolate turtles and peanut-butter fudge. There was the town hall, with the library across the street where Sam had found Harris Stoughton's book. I smelled the delicious aroma coming from Rocconi's Pizzeria on Middle Street, where she used to meet her friends after school. And at the old floral shop on Main Street, the window was filled with lilacs—her favorite flower. It was all so strange, so unreal. I felt so close to her. For the first time in a long while, I missed her with a physical ache.

It began to rain again, catching us completely off guard. It wasn't a warning trickle that led to a bigger downpour—it was like thousands of buckets had been kicked over at once, sudden and freezing. Charlie grabbed my elbow and steered me down the street through the rain into a nearby coffee bar. We squished up to the counter and surveyed the offerings. When I reached for my purse, Charlie held up his hand.

"Please," he said. "It's on me. What do you like?"

"Thanks," I said. "Just coffee. Lots of milk and sugar."

"Got it," he said.

I snagged a cozy table by the window with two plush seats and sat down to consider the significance of his action. No guy I knew had ever just bought things for me. I didn't even know that many people who were bought things on dates. What was *this* about? You don't buy coffees for someone you don't like, right? Charlie must like me. Not *like me,* like me—but he could tolerate me. Or so it seemed.

I occupied myself with this stupid internal dialogue until he came over a few minutes later with two grotesquely large mugs of frothy something and two biscotti wrapped in a napkin.

"What are these?" I said, accepting one of the heaping cups with a smile of thanks.

"I have no idea," he said, poking suspiciously at the foam, as if he was testing to see if it was alive. "Grande cappu-frappes or something. I told them to make something big and steamy, with lots of milk. They gave me these. I'm assuming they're coffees."

He held up his foamy stirrer and grimaced theatrically. I had to laugh.

We sat in the coffee shop for hours, talking. Usually I'm not great around people I don't know very well. I'm that shy girl, the one who goes through a crisis every time she even has to ask someone where the ladies' room is in a restaurant. So my ease around Charlie was odd. For some reason, I felt like I could talk to him about anything. I loved the way he could be so serious, and then something funny would occur to him, and he'd half jump from his seat and lean forward in excitement, his whole face bursting. During one story he became so animated that he knocked the sugar canister off the table three times.

"So," I said, continuing our conversation from the walk, "your dad's some kind of genius?"

"More or less," he said. "He's a number theorist. He's

your classic absentminded professor. Brilliant beyond belief, but he literally forgets to feed himself."

"And you ended up finishing high school early? You must be pretty smart yourself."

"It's not a big deal," he said, stirring what was left of his coffee. "I did well, but it was nothing exciting. And my dad's been a really, really good math tutor."

"What about your mom?" I asked.

"Oh"—he shrugged uncomfortably—"she died a few years ago."

"Sorry," I said, understanding his reaction. "My mom died, too, and I hate having to explain to people. They always give you the *look*. It's kind of sympathetic, but mostly it's really nervous. It's like they think they've torn open a wound, and you're going to start screaming or something."

"That's the one," he said, grinning thankfully.

"So you must spend a lot of time alone, then," I said.

"No." He shook his head. "I spend a lot of time with Brigid and her family. I have a standing invitation to dinner every single night, which is nice."

He put his feet up on the empty chair at our table and leaned back to look at me.

"So," he said, "what about you? Your dad doesn't know anything about Wicca at all?"

"He knows that it freaks him out," I said. "That's about it. I'm sure he just thinks it's some kind of phase I'm going through. A better-Wicca-than-drugs kind of a thing, I guess."

"If he doesn't like Wicca, why did he let you come here?"

"Um . . . my dad doesn't exactly know where I am," I confessed.

"What does that mean?" he asked, one eyebrow arching.

"It means I ran away."

Okay. There. Someone knew. I twirled my biscotti in the dregs of my coffee foam as nonchalantly as I could, wondering if Charlie was going to jump up and start yelling for the cops. Instead, he exhaled and leaned back into the red velvet seat.

"Why?" he asked calmly.

"A lot of reasons. Mostly because things were happening to me—I was having dreams about this place. My mother's Book of Shadows appeared out of nowhere. Sam's letters fell out of a broken box. So I wrote to you, and I made contact. It all felt like it was meant to be."

"And, of course, you couldn't tell your dad about any of it."

"Right," I said, running my hands through my hair. "There were other reasons, too. . . ."

"Like what?"

"I have powers," I said. "They came on all of a sudden and kind of freaked me out."

He dropped his feet down to the floor and leaned in to me.

"How's that possible?" he said, his eyes glowing with wonder. "Your father's not a witch, and your mother . . ." He stopped himself and shook his head. "Wow. I'm an *ass.* I can't believe I just said that. Sorry."

"It's all right," I said, waving my hand dismissively. "I know it's weird. My coven leader's father thinks it might be that since my mother stripped herself of her powers, they were all somehow concentrated in me. I definitely have more than I can handle. They tend to do things on their own. The last thing I did before running away was cause some kind of water explosion in my coven leader's house. We were doing a release spell to get rid of negative emotions, and . . ."

I hung my head. Charlie was so experienced—I was a moron. Still, he was listening attentively, and I knew I could tell him what had happened to me. Again, don't ask me why.

". . . I almost flooded his house. It was awful. It was the most embarrassing moment of my life, and that's saying something. I just started crying, and I couldn't stop."

He was quiet for a minute. I couldn't raise my head. I just stared into the table.

"Trust me," he said, "I know how difficult and embarrassing it can be when you're first trying to use your power. Everyone screws up. All witches know this."

"I can't imagine the people who run my coven screwing up," I replied, envisioning all of the experienced blood witches I knew—Hunter, Sky, Mr. Niall. They were probably born cool, calm, and talented. And sure, Morgan was erratic, but she was also superpowerful, and I'd seen some of the wonders she was capable of when we'd put our minds together. I was just regular and inept.

"They did," he said with conviction. "I promise you. I know I was a master at it."

He could see I doubted him.

"I'll give you an example," he offered. "A lot of covens get together to hold circles and lessons for preinitiates. Our assignment one week was a simple nochd. A nochd is a revealing spell. Our teachers would hide something, and we would each use the spell to find it. When I was a kid, I always used to try to prove to everyone how smart I was. I wanted to do the most amazing and complicated nochd in the group. I searched through all of our books for a whole week. I finally found one that was hundreds of years old that I was sure no one else would have. I can still remember it. It was very long and involved. Everyone was impressed. Unfortunately, what I didn't realize is that not all nochds are alike. The term has many meanings, and the spells have many purposes. I wasn't smart enough to figure that out until it was too late."

"What happened?" I asked, looking up with interest.

"Just as I came to the end, silence. Everyone just stared at me. I mean, *stared*. And then they all started to laugh. Then I realized that the room had gotten really cold."

"Did you do some kind of weather spell?" I asked.

"A nochd," he said with a grin, "is also a spell for naked-ness, a complete revealing of self."

I gasped with sudden laughter and put my hand over my mouth.

"Well," Charlie went on, "because I was young and dumb, I didn't realize right away that I was standing in front of my friends completely naked. I was so busy looking around to see what I had revealed that it took me a second to look down at myself to see what people were staring at."

"But aren't Wiccans okay with that?" I asked, still laugh-ing. "I mean, being naked?"

"Sure," he said. "It won't get you in trouble. But we were still just a bunch of thirteen-year-olds. And being thirteen and naked in front of all your friends, both male and female—that's the same for everyone."

"What did you do?" I asked.

"I froze," he said. "I had *no idea* what to do. One of the teachers quickly undid the spell, but I was standing there long enough for everyone to get a nice long look at me. There I was: brilliant, naked Charlie."

He didn't seem to mind that I was rolling with laughter over stories of his childhood traumas. He even took a little bow.

"So messing up is one thing. The real trouble comes when you're just trying to impress people with magick you don't know how to control. Like what Brigid was trying to do back at the restaurant," he said, looking directly into my eyes, "before you stopped her."

I almost fell out of my chair. Even though it happened again and again, sometimes I just couldn't get used to the fact that other witches always seemed to know what you were doing and thinking.

"I—I didn't . . ." I stammered. "I mean, I did, but I wasn't trying to embarrass her. . . ."

"No," he said, waving his hand. "It's all right. It was a good thing that you did. It could have been dangerous."

"How did you know?" I said.

"I felt your energy coming out. I could sense it redirecting hers."

Funny. He and I could both sense energy, but Brigid didn't appear to be able to. I wondered if something was wrong with her powers. Maybe they were weak. Maybe that was why she was trying to prove herself so much.

"How did you do it, exactly?" Charlie asked. "What spell was that?"

"I don't know," I replied, shaking my head. "It just kind of came to me. I did this thing about a week ago . . . a *tàth meànma* . . . something. . . . I kind of locked minds with someone, a very powerful witch."

"A *tàth meànma brach?*" he said, his eyes wide.

"That was it. I didn't realize it at the time, but I just kind of . . . learned things, I guess. When I saw what Brigid was doing, I was afraid, and I wanted to stop her. Suddenly it was as if I heard my friend's voice somewhere deep in my mind. I just knew what to do."

Charlie was staring at me as if I had just sprouted wings and a beak.

"What?" I asked anxiously, looking myself over. "What did I do?"

"You did a *brach?*" he repeated.

"Is that weird?" I asked, feeling myself hunch down in my chair.

"No . . ." he said, pulling absently at a handful of his loopy curls. "Well, not in a bad way. It's rare. And difficult. And dangerous. Why did you do a *brach?*"

"Oh. It wasn't my idea—it was my coven leader's, and he's crazy careful. He's a Seeker."

"Your coven leader is a Seeker?"

"Yeah." I nodded vigorously. "He's the youngest Seeker. He's nineteen."

Charlie stopped speaking. His mouth just hung open slightly. He waited for me to go on.

"There was an emergency," I said. "Something really bad had happened, and they needed me to help with a spell. The only way I could do it was by getting information from my friend. So we did a *tàth meànma brach.*"

Charlie sat and silently contemplated this for a moment. I glanced up at the clock. It was six-ten.

"We're late," I said, alarmed. "It's after six."

He nodded, still deep in thought, and we grabbed our

things and ran out toward his car. The rain was coming down hard, and the streets were full of foggy mist. After we slithered, soaking, disgusting wet into the car, I turned to him. His hair was dark, and one or two of the curls clung to his face very attractively. I wanted to ask him something, but the sight of him made my tongue go all numb.

"What's up?" he said, immediately sensing my question. He brushed some of the water from his face and rummaged around in the glove compartment. He produced a handful of tissues, which we used to dry off.

"Are you coming tonight, or are you just dropping me off?" I asked quickly. He looked up with interest.

"I could come," he said. "Why? Can't get enough of my amazing company?"

"Sort of." I laughed. "It's just that Evelyn . . . my grand-mother . . . she doesn't seem to like me. She seems angry that I'm here. It would be nice to have a friendly face."

This didn't seem to shock Charlie.

"Sure," he said. "I'd be happy to come. I'll help you get through it."

Though I must have looked like hell, I felt about a million times better as we headed back toward the house.

11

Shatter

July 30, 1951

Father died of a heart attack five days ago. It came on suddenly, and no one was at home. Nothing could be done.

Hugh and I have stopped looking for a house. We will live here. Mother will need support and help with Tioma. To make matters worse, this has stirred up Oona. She shredded the curtains in the living room and broke the panes of glass in our front door. Mother and I watched as it happened. She wept endlessly. I need to be strong.

Goddess, I know you give, and I know you must take. I revere you, though my heart is broken.

—Aoibheann

"I came along," Charlie said, peeling off his sopping jacket as we stepped into the foyer. "I hope that's all right."

"Of course," Ruth said with a smile. "Always. I'll set another place."

"I'll get it," he said, slipping back toward the kitchen. "Don't worry about it, Ruth."

Ruth nodded, looking at me kindly. "Alisa, the bathroom is right by the front door. You can wash your hands and dry off a bit in there."

"Thanks," I said. Ruth returned to the kitchen, and I found the powder room, which was just big enough to fit a toilet and a very small sink. I looked like a drowned rat. My hair was completely soaked, and it clung to my head. My clothes were getting really swampy. There were beeswax soap and a jar of salt crystals for washing hands. I used both, rubbing the crystals into my skin anxiously, as if I could impress my grandmother by having the cleanest hands of anyone she'd ever met. By the time I came out, I'd turned my hands red from the effort, and everyone was gathered in the dining room, waiting for me.

The room was filled by a long oval-shaped table and a massive sideboard, both of which looked like they were probably well over a century old. The table was heavy with food, served up on delicate pieces of blue-and-white china. There was an incredible-smelling roast, with big bowls of fluffy potatoes, asparagus, and roasted carrots. The gravy was so thick and aromatic that it had to be completely homemade, and the soft biscuits were already dripping with butter. From what I'd seen so far, the Curtises were very good cooks.

We all sat down. I had been put next to Sam. Charlie set his place next to Brigid. Evelyn and Ruth had the opposite ends. With a snap of her fingers Evelyn lit the two tall taper candles in silver candlesticks. I had a feeling that little trick was for my benefit.

"When are you returning home, Alisa?" Evelyn asked me, rather properly, as she passed Ruth the potatoes. Nice. I'd just gotten here, and she wanted to know when I was leaving.

"In . . . a few days," I said. "It's my spring break."

"Well," said Sam, "I hope you can stay for our circle on Wednesday. It's our annual celebration of the founding of Ròiseal. We're getting together the night before as well, for Ruth's birthday. It's a big week."

"Yeah," Brigid agreed. "You have to come."

"I'd like that," I said, not really sure if that was true. Sam, Charlie, Brigid, and Ruth were great—but Evelyn was so seriously scary that I had to wonder how long I really wanted to stay here. Well, at least the circle on Wednesday gave me something to plan around.

Evelyn said nothing, just eyed the progress of the food around the table. When everyone had filled their plates, she nodded, and I saw the others take up their silverware. I followed suit. My mother hadn't mentioned how formal the family dinners were. She probably hadn't noticed. Unlike me, she'd had no Hilary leaving the table to barf every fifteen minutes. She had no basis for comparison.

Evelyn started talking again but to everyone but me. She asked Charlie about school, his job, his father, and his plans for college. She asked Brigid if anything interesting had happened at the shop and how her training was going.

"Brigid has been training with a healer," Sam explained to me, attempting to include me in the conversation.

"That's great," I said to Brigid, who smiled proudly. "Do you need to do a lot of studying?"

"Some," she said. "A lot of it is exercises in channeling energy. Then you add the herbs and the oils, but only after you learn to feel out the problem or the injury."

"You wouldn't understand, Alisa," Evelyn said, turning to me. "It involves magick."

Charlie looked over at me meaningfully. I could tell he was wondering if one of us should tell them about my powers. I shook my head quickly. I really didn't want to get into it with them. He got the message and opted to change the course of the conversation.

"So," he said, "you're from Texas, right?" I'd just told him that this afternoon.

"That's right," I said, breaking open a steamy biscuit. "That's where I was born. We lived there until recently."

"How do you like the winters up here?" Sam asked cheerfully.

"I don't," I said with a smile, "except for the snow. I like snow, but my father can't drive in it. He never learned how. So if it even flurries, my future stepmonst—mother has to drive. If she's not home, we're stuck."

A polite chuckle from everyone but Evelyn, who was communing with her roasted carrots. Sam, Ruth, Charlie, and Brigid continued to ask me questions about my life. For the most part they were just making polite conversation, not going into anything too deeply. Evelyn pointedly said nothing. I noticed all of the others giving her sideways glances, but these didn't seem to penetrate her steely exterior. She wasn't interested in talking to me. Period.

I had just finished telling them a little about my dad's job and my grandparents in Buenos Aires when Evelyn suddenly lifted her head and focused on me, hard and fast.

"How does your father feel about the craft?" she said.

"The craft?" I repeated. "You mean Wicca?"

"I do."

"I don't think he's happy about my involvement with it," I answered honestly. "But he doesn't really know that much about it. I think he assumes it's a fad at our high school."

"A *fad* at your high school?"

"A lot of my friends are in my coven," I explained, gripping my silverware fearfully. "He just knows that's where I go on Saturdays. We rotate hosting the circle, although I probably won't be hosting one. I bring snacks, though."

"Snacks are good," Sam said with a nod. "Witches love snacks, especially sweets."

"So you contribute snacks at Wicca circles," she said.

This was a blatant twisting of my words, designed to make me look like a fool. I couldn't believe it. It was so unnecessary, this quietly vicious behavior. She was so composed, passing around her roast and her gravy and just stinging the hell out of her granddaughter. Around me I felt these little tendrils of emotion as the others reached out to me. That was nice of them, but it didn't really take away the painful reality of the situation.

Then, in with those gestures of sympathy, something else came along. It wasn't in words, and it wasn't in sound—but somehow it was as clear as if someone was shouting into my ear.

Something's wrong.

What the hell was that? A vicious chill ran all through my body, as if someone had just plugged an IV of ice water into my veins. There was a creaking sound and a snap of wind. Before I knew what was happening, Charlie jumped up and pushed Brigid away from the table.

"Ruth!" he shouted, throwing out his hand and pointing at her. A bolt of energy, pale white, came from his hand and threw Ruth back toward the wall. In the same second all the lights in the room went out in a cloud of electric sparks as the chandelier above us broke free and crashed down onto the table, shattering glass and splintering wood. The snapped wires danced above our heads like angry snakes, still pulsing with current. Evelyn, already on her feet, held up her hand and made them still. With another flash of movement she deadened the sparks that still came from the chandelier. Now all was dark, and acrid burning smells hung in the air.

"Is everyone all right?" Charlie called.

"I am," I said, my voice shaking. "Sam is."

Evelyn snapped to light some candles on the sideboard. I could see that Ruth had been thrown far enough to spare her head, but her arms had still been too close. The thing had come down on them, pinning her to the table. Brigid was by her mother's side, crying, mumbling spells that had no visible effect. Ruth looked like she was in too much pain to speak. Her face was covered in tiny bloody trails, probably slices from the flying glass.

Sam joined Charlie, who had uttered a quick spell that seemed to make the heavy, tinkling fixture a little easier to lift. They gingerly moved it away from Ruth, taking great pains not to further her injury. Brigid started running her hands over Ruth, obviously trying to do some healing work, but Evelyn came and took her shoulder.

"Go start the car, Brigid," she said. "She needs to go to the hospital. Charlie, can you carry her?"

Charlie nodded and ran for his jacket.

"I think we should call the council," Sam said. "This has gone far enough."

"I know a Seeker," I found myself saying. "If I called him, he could be here in a few hours."

Evelyn looked up at Sam and looked in my direction.

"I think you'd better leave," she said. "We'll take her to the hospital."

Charlie came back in just in time to catch the tail end of this conversation. His eyebrows rose, and his naturally cheerful expression faded into one of surprised disgust. I had a feeling that if the situation hadn't been so dire, he might have even spoken up on my behalf. But this wasn't the time. He bent down and picked Ruth up in a cradle lift. She quietly wept in pain and fear, and I heard him reassuring her as he took her through the hall to the door.

Sam, thunderstruck at our dismissal, stood there staring at his mother. She turned on her heel and followed Charlie down the hall. Sam put his arm around my shoulders and led me through the front door. We stood on the porch and watched as Brigid pulled out and sped the car down the street and out of sight. Sam quietly pulled a key from his pocket and locked the door.

"Are you sure you're all right?" he said.

"I'm fine," I assured him. "What about you?"

"It could have killed her," he said, instead of answering what I had asked. "Thank the Goddess Charlie's quick."

We got into his car. For a moment Sam just sat in the driver's seat, hands on the steering wheel, looking too tense to put the key in the ignition.

"Evelyn seemed so angry when I mentioned calling a Seeker," I said. "Why?"

"Not everyone likes the council," he answered, his expression dark. I got the feeling this was a regular bone of contention. "Some people are offended that one group of witches should take it upon themselves to govern other witches, to pass judgment. I think the council has done some very good work. We could use their help."

He sighed, beat a little rhythm onto the steering wheel,

then started the car. I looked out at the people walking along the beach path and heading to the pubs for the evening. Apparently some people in this town had normal lives.

"Charlie and Brigid told me about Oona," I said. Sam glanced over at me.

"They did?" he said. "Good. I was wondering how to explain what just happened."

"Stuff like that has happened before?" I asked.

"This was the worst so far," he replied. "But the phenomena have been getting more serious just lately. It certainly seems like my mother wants to wait until someone gets killed before she'll ask for help."

His undercurrent of rage was palpable, so I fell silent and let him have a few minutes to think things over.

"I'm sorry, Alisa," he said just as we pulled into his driveway. "I'm sorry about the way your grandmother treated you. I don't even know what to say about it."

"It's like you said, I guess," I answered, trying to be diplomatic. "It's just strange to have me show up."

"Still, she has no right to behave like that. I just want you to know that she and I feel very differently about your being here. You can stay with me as long as you like—and as long as your dad lets you."

This triggered my memory. Twenty-four hours . . . the watch sigil on my neck. I had to call Morgan.

"Oh," I said, as casually as I could, "would it be all right if I used your phone? I just need to check in. It's long distance, but I'll be quick."

"Take your time," Sam said. "I'm sure your dad would like an update."

A strange expression crossed his face, but I decided not to

try to read into it too much. For all I knew, Sam had been onto me from the first.

"I leave for work pretty early in the morning," he said. "Sleep in. I'll leave you keys so you can come and go as you please. I'll be home around five. We'll do something different tomorrow night, like see a movie."

"Thanks," I said. "That would be great."

Astrophe and Mandu pounced on us the moment we stepped in the door. Sam fed them, then went upstairs. I took the phone into the kitchen for privacy. I got lucky. Morgan answered, not Mary K.

"It's me," I said. "Alisa. I know I'm almost out of time, but I made it."

"Oh, hi . . ." she said casually. I heard her quickly moving into a quieter place and shutting a door. "Alisa," she said in a low voice, "how are you? Is everything okay?"

"Um," I said hesitantly. "A little weird, actually. My uncle is great. My grandmother looks at me like I'm an escaped convict that's hiding in her house. And there's some kind of killer ghost on the loose. . . ."

"What?"

I told her the grim tale as it had unfolded so far.

"You were right," she said. "Something weird was definitely going on up there. Do you think this is what the dreams were about?"

"I don't know," I said as Astrophe leaped into my lap. "I'm going to have to stay here a few more days to find out. I figure I have spring-break week, at least. So, how bad is it down there?"

"Well," she said with a sigh, "your dad is upset. Frantic,

actually. He called here about an hour after I got back." My stomach turned. "I also told Hunter what happened," she continued. "He understands what you're doing, but he's really worried, too. He'll be glad to know you called."

I had to promise to call back soon before she let me get off the phone. You can always get out of something your parents try to make you do, but when a powerful witch puts a sigil on your neck, you're pretty much stuck.

A while later, after I had settled down for the night on Sam's couch and was flipping through my mother's Book of Shadows in preparation for going to sleep, the phone rang. After a minute Sam called down for me to pick up the phone.

"Hey," said a voice. "Sorry to be calling so late."

It was Charlie. He sounded tired, and I could hear him climbing into bed as he spoke. Thank God he couldn't see me—I was grinning like an idiot. Charlie was calling for me!

"I just thought you might like to know," he went on, "Ruth's arm is broken, but she's okay otherwise. Banged up and upset, of course, but intact."

"I—I'm glad," I said, stuttering in my excitement. "I mean, I'm glad that she'll be all right."

"What about you?" he asked.

"What about me? It didn't land on me."

"The chandelier didn't, no," he said. "But that whole dinner was kind of rough."

"Oh. I'm fine," I said, pretty unconvincingly. "No problem."

"I guess you haven't realized yet that it's pretty much useless to lie to witches," he said.

Actually, that much I had figured out on my own. I knew that most other witches could read me like a book. But what surprised me was that I could read him as well, and his concern amazed me—it was deep. Deep to the point that I could feel it all the way across the town, physically, as if a warm embrace could travel down a telephone line. "It wasn't the welcome I wanted," I confessed. "But it was nice that you were there. Thanks for coming."

He let the line go quiet for a moment. He didn't try to tell me that it would all be fine, because it didn't appear that it would be.

"What are you doing tomorrow?" he asked.

"Sam's working," I said, throwing my legs over the top of the couch and hanging upside down. "I don't know. Staying here, I guess. I don't think Evelyn wants to have me over again anytime soon."

"Want some company? We're on spring break, too, and I have the day off from the shop."

A *whole day* with Charlie? I couldn't think of anything I wanted more. But was that weird? This was my cousin's boyfriend. Should I be spending that much time with him?

"What about Brigid?" I asked. "Doesn't she have off from school, too?"

"She does," he said, "but she's working." When I didn't answer right away, he came back a little nervously. "We don't have to," he said. "I just thought . . ."

What the hell was wrong with me? Just because Charlie made me weak at the knees didn't mean that he was going to ditch my cousin to run off with me.

"No, no," I backpedaled quickly. "I want to. I mean, I'd like to. Actually, I'd like to do some research on my background. There's a lot of stuff I have questions about, family stuff. There's a library my mom keeps talking about in her Book of Shadows. It's in the house. That would be perfect, but it sounds like it's secret."

"Research!" he said. "That I can help you with. As for the library, I've never seen it, but I'm sure there is one. All Rowanwands have a collection of books somewhere, and as head of the coven, I'm sure Evelyn has thousands of books. The door is probably spelled, so you can't see it unless someone shows you where it is. I'll bet we can find it. It might take a while, but it can be done."

"How?"

"Spells leave traces. There'll be runes or sigils to mark the doorway. We'll just need to narrow down the area of the house where to look because it can take a long time to find them. Does she say anything about where it might be?"

By now I knew the book almost by heart, and I automatically flipped through to the pages that mentioned the family library.

"Well," I said, finding a page, "she says one time that she was writing in the study, and then she went down to the library."

"So it's in the basement," he said. "Great. That's where we'll start."

"Start?"

"We're going to go in there and find it," he said matter-of-factly. "If Evelyn's not willing to help you, I am. I'll pick you up first thing in the morning."

12

Revealing

Mabon, 1952

Five years of scrying for Oona have been fruitless. Every spell has been tried and retried. There is only one other option: I must open a bith dearc, an opening to the land of the dead. This is a difficult and dangerous procedure, but it is the only option left that I can see. I have been researching this process for over a year, and I feel that it is time to proceed.

Tioma wants me to ask the council's permission. The council? Who are the council but a bunch of busybodies with nothing better to do than to pry into the business of others? Their time would be better spent honing their own craft. As a witch and as a Rowanwand, I take responsibility for my own decisions and actions.

The need is real. Oona is trapped here, and she must be released, for all of our sakes. By opening the dearc, we may be able to provide her with a channel through which she can return to the spirit world. The ceremony will take place in two days' time, *when the moon is full. Great care has been taken to restrict the spell, so it must be written with absolute precision. Claire Findgoll has been assisting me in this task. Her collection of books on lunar spellcraft and spell restrictions is unparalleled.*

I had planned on telling Mother about the dearc, but she has not been well recently, and I do not want to worry her. Better that she remain unaware.

—Aoibheann

I woke up to the sound of the door shutting. I heard a car engine start and the sound of the car pulling off down the street. Sam was gone, off to work. Astrophe and Mandu were tangled together and sleeping in the space between my back and the sofa. Carefully, so as not to disturb them, I slipped out from under the afghan.

I wanted to be completely ready whenever Charlie showed up, and I had no idea when that would be. I rushed into the tiny bathroom and took a shower. It was obvious when I went through my bag that I had been pretty distracted when I packed. Eight pairs of underwear, three sets of pajamas, three bras, and one T-shirt. No clean socks or pants. Good job, Alisa. I pulled on the T-shirt and grabbed the socks, jeans, and hooded sweater that I'd been wearing for the last thirty-six hours and did my best to fix myself up a bit.

Dressing complete, I headed to the kitchen. On the table I found the keys, a neat list of local points of interest, a small hand-drawn map, and a note with Sam's work number. I made myself some scrambled eggs and toast and turned on a morning talk show. I was just coming to the exciting con-clusion of a discussion on new trends in lighting fixtures when the doorbell rang. Through the curtain I could see the little green Volkswagen out on the street.

Panic. Did I have jam on my face? Would he notice that I was basically wearing the same outfit, which was still kind of nasty from the day before? No time to do anything about that now. I opened the door.

Charlie had on a well-worn fisherman's sweater, and his hair was still slightly shower damp, which brought out the curls. He was waiting on the step, holding out two paper cups from the shop that we'd stopped at yesterday.

"Coffee," he said, smiling and holding one out to me. "Four sugars. Extra milk."

"Perfect, thanks." I eagerly accepted the cup. "What happens now?" I asked after I'd had a sip. "How do we know when everyone at Evelyn's house will be out?"

"They're out now," he said. "I checked. Ruth and Brigid are both working. Evelyn went to Boston for the day. She meets with other witches there once a week to study new divination spells. We can leave whenever you're ready."

"Are you sure about this?" I asked, suddenly feeling a little nervous.

"Completely," he said.

We headed out to his car. Operation Find the Library was under way.

We parked well down the street from the house and walked back. Charlie casually did these little spells he called see-me-nots, which he assured me would keep us from being noticed by anyone.

"So," I said with a nervous grin as we stood on the porch of Evelyn's house, "how do we get in? Magick?"

"Yup." He smiled back, reaching into his pocket. He fished around for a moment and produced a key. "Ta da!"

I shook my head in mock disgust.

"This is my key," he admitted. "I'm pretty much allowed to come and go as I like. I fix the computer, shovel the snow, get herbs from the garden. I pretty much live here half the time. Getting in won't be quite as exciting as I might have made it sound."

"Please," I said as he unlocked the door. "Give me boring any day. I have enough excitement in my life."

Just as a precaution, Charlie called into the house to see if anyone was home. When there was no reply, we slipped inside and locked the door behind us. The house was still and sunny. We hurried to the basement door, which was in the kitchen. A narrow, steep flight of stairs led into the unfinished basement. The low-ceilinged space was full of snow shovels, sleds, old boots, and a few well-organized sets of shelves holding ordinary household items like flowerpots and bags of potting soil. There was a rickety old toboggan in the corner and a small box with a badminton set.

I was tingling from the moment we entered this part of the house. It seemed as if my mother's presence hadn't been washed clean from here. Some of these things, I knew, were hers. Even though it was rather strange and painful, I felt my senses expanding, as if I was growing stronger with her energy. There was something down here that seemed to be screaming out to me.

"It's here," I said suddenly.

He looked back at me.

"You feel it?" he said.

"Yeah," I replied, looking around for some sign of a doorway. Unless they were keeping it in an old box under the lawn darts, I didn't see anywhere they could be hiding a library in this place.

"Okay," he said, glancing around, too. "We've got to move all of this away from the walls."

With a quick motion he pulled off his sweater. Underneath he was wearing a dark blue T-shirt printed with just one word: FRED. I noticed that his arms were covered in very light freckles as well and that they were surprisingly well defined. I guessed he did more than just work on math problems, or else he had some really heavy pencils. Then I decided to stop gawking at his arms and look like I was actually there to help. I pulled off my sweater as well and threw it down with his.

Together we shifted everything away from the wall by at least a foot or two. When we were done, Charlie pulled his athame out of his messenger bag. It was entirely made of highly polished silver, with a Celtic engraving around the handle and a round piece of black onyx set at the very top. Slowly, working right under the ceiling, he ran the athame around the walls, moving down a bit every time he made a complete pass. He had to go around about two dozen times to cover the whole area.

When that revealed nothing, he started on the floor, passing the athame carefully over every inch. He had to stop every few minutes so that we could rearrange the furniture. Again nothing. He straightened up and stared down at the floor, puzzled. Then he slouched against the wall and squinted around with an intent expression, tapping his athame in his palm.

"I have an idea," he finally said. "But it involves both of us. It's possible that because you're a blood relative, the door will be revealed to you more easily. So together we're going to do a nochd."

"Should I close my eyes?" I said, keeping a very straight face.

"I expected that," he replied with a wry grin. "Here." He held out the athame to me, handle first.

I pointed to the athame. "Can I . . . hold that? I mean, is it *sacred* or something?"

"Well," he said, "it's a magickal tool—so, yes. It's sacred. But it belongs to me, and I have no problem with you using it. Whether or not it works pretty much depends on you. Magickal tools function when the user brings their magick to them."

"You mean, like the toaster only works when you plug it in? Then it can use its bread-charring powers."

"Exactly." He nodded with a smile. "The tool is the toaster. You're the socket."

I accepted the athame, and he fished through his bag and removed a white candle and a piece of chalk.

"I'll cast the spell," he said. "We're going to see if your energy can guide us. I'll lead you as we go, so don't worry."

"Okay," I agreed, feeling weird with the heavy athame in my hand. "How do I hold it? Up, or down, or out . . ."

"Just let your arm fall naturally by your side," he said, expertly drawing a circle around us. Then he placed the candle in the middle, between us, and drew a series of runes around it in chalk. Standing, he lightly took hold of my right wrist, gripping just below the handle of the athame. He flashed me a look to see if I was ready, and I nodded.

"*Aingeal*," he intoned.

The candle snapped to life. I guess I shouldn't have been so startled. I'd seen both Morgan and Evelyn do that. Still, to see Charlie do it surprised me.

"*Sinn sir ni keillit*," he continued. The metal of the athame grew warm. He tightened his grip on my wrist—not enough to hurt me, but enough to have a firm grasp. "*Tar er ash, seòl heen.*"

I saw now why he had tightened his hold. My arm began to quake, and for a moment I thought I might drop the athame. He locked his hand around mine and looked down at me. Magick was flowing through us, between us. I could feel his strength as he controlled its flow. I'm not sure if it was the magick or simply being so close to him, but my heart started beating like crazy. It seemed so loud that I actually thought he would be able to hear it.

In one movement our arms rose together—mine started to come forward, pushing his back. I was pointing the athame to a spot on the floor. He couldn't see it because it was behind him, but a square appeared in that spot. It was made of symbols, very finely drawn in a bluish light. I wanted to say something, but I thought it might ruin the spell. As it was, he seemed aware that something was happening, even though he couldn't see what I saw.

Giving thanks to the Goddess and the God, he ended the spell, but he held on to my hand for a moment. We said nothing—just stood there, looking at each other. I felt the warmth of his body and could smell the faint smell of laundry detergent, some kind of spicy men's deodorant, and faint traces of sage smoke. Charlie smell. So nice. As he gazed down at me, I realized that he was the only person who could really stare at me like that without my wanting to turn away or hide my face. I could actually look him right in the eye and not flinch. Even though his expression was serious and intent, his mouth still retained its wide, happy curve. It was as if he was born to smile and to make others smile. Such a nice mouth.

Such a *what?* What was I thinking?

Unintentionally I pulled away. He backed up, as though I'd startled him. His face was flushed, and he didn't seem to know where to look for a moment.

"There's a . . . thing on the floor," I mumbled, pointing.

"Good!" he said, quickly kneeling down and snapping out the candle flame with his fingers. "That's what was supposed to happen. We did it. Good work."

I brushed the chalk circle away as Charlie sprawled flat on the floor to examine the symbols up close. I saw him working his way all around the square. By now my mind was everywhere it shouldn't be. I could see only the length of his body, the way the sleeves of his T-shirt tightened around his upper arms, the speed of his movements.

Cousin's boyfriend, I kept saying to myself over and over and over.

"Okay," he said, getting up to his knees, "this shouldn't be too bad. Finding it was the hard part. The seal itself isn't a tremendous piece of work." He reached back for his bag and started rooting through it again, producing a handful of runes.

"Have you got a whole magick shop in there?" I asked.

"No, ma'am," he said. "Just the basics. Some candles, chalk, athame, runes. All the things witches should never travel without, especially when they're trying to break into other witches' private libraries."

I gulped, feeling a pang of guilt as he set a rune in each corner of the box, then put the white candle in the center. He muttered a spell quietly to himself. The candle winked to life again, and over the next few minutes, as he spelled and tapped his athame around its perimeter, the dusty patch of floor revealed itself to be a wooden door with a round handle.

"Voilà," he said, looking up in satisfaction. "One trapdoor."

"That was amazing," I told him, completely awed. "You're like a safecracker." He didn't reply, just gave a nervous little laugh.

When we opened the wooden door, we found a switch that turned on a set of overhead lights. They revealed a set of tiny steps that dropped almost straight down into a darker room. Charlie went down first, then offered up his hand to help me down. He had to bend down, as the low ceiling didn't give him much clearance.

You'd think a room under a house like this would be musty and dirty, but it was spotlessly clean. The walls and floor were made of smooth stone. There were an air filter and a dehumidifier. Every inch of space was carefully utilized. The walls were completely set with shelves, and several freestanding floor-to-ceiling bookcases sat back to back in eight rows. The pathways between the rows of books were narrow, just large enough for a person to pass through with a step stool. In one corner there was a small antique reading table with a lamp and two chairs.

"This place is *great,*" he said, his expression melting into one of amazement at the sight of all the books. It was like watching a little kid at an amusement park, so deliriously excited that they don't know where to head first. In his enthusiasm he stumbled but caught himself on one of the bookcases.

"It's my ballet training coming through," he said with a smile as his face turned charmingly pink. Then he bounded off into the stacks.

As Charlie devoured the titles on the shelves, I walked around quietly, taking in the magnitude and splendor of the collection. Many of the books, though ancient, weren't particularly frail. They'd been so well taken care of that age had affected them only slightly. There were books in strange blocky print, dating well back into the 1600s. There were books in all kinds of languages, in mysterious prints and symbols. Some sections were full of dry, academic-sounding titles. Others were filled with books so exotic looking that I was actually frightened to touch them.

As I turned down one aisle, it was as if the books were whispering to me. I glanced over their titles. I couldn't read any of them. They looked like German to me, lots of huge words starting with *das* or *der*. Still, even though I couldn't understand them, I wanted to touch them. I wanted to pull them from the shelves. I wanted—this one—*Edelsteine und Metalle,* whatever that meant. I *needed* this book. Gently I slipped it from the shelf. It seemed warm to the touch, as if I'd been holding it for a long time. Surprisingly there was nothing on the front cover. It was a plain green book, covered in cloth, obviously very old. I flipped it back and looked at the spine again, but I now saw nothing written there.

I almost dropped the book in shock.

"Charlie!" I called, my voice husky.

He came right around from the row behind. I explained

what I had seen and offered the book to him. He took it, examined it all over.

"*Edelsteine und Metalle*," he said, holding the spine out for me to see. "Something and metals."

I looked at the spine again. There was the title, in gold letters on the greenish black cloth. It hadn't been there a second ago. I was shaking a bit now, and he put his hand on my shoulder to steady me.

"It must have been spelled with some kind of glamor or concealment spell," he said. "That's all. You're not going crazy. Let's have a look at it and find out why it was being hidden. This is a private family library, so it's kind of strange for a Rowanwand to hide a book from a relative."

We took it over to the reading table and switched on the light. Charlie began to page through the book. In the first moment we could see that it was definitely not a German textbook on something and metals. It was handwritten, in English. It looked like a Book of Shadows, with dates at the tops of the pages. Charlie's eyes grew wider with every page.

"This is Máirín's book," he said, looking up, his eyes full of awe. "Oona's daughter. No one's seen this book in years. How the hell . . ."

Máirín's book. That was what I had found. The story of the family witch, down here, in the secret Curtis family library. This was where my mother had experienced a frightening telekinetic episode. There was too much magick, too many feelings tied into this house. I chose this moment to become completely overwhelmed. Even though I tried to will them back, I felt tears well up behind my eyes. Charlie looked up in alarm and saw my eyes glistening.

"What is it?" he said, setting his hand back on my shoulder.

"All these weird feelings," I answered, rubbing my eyes. "All of these strange things I don't understand."

As much as I knew he was dying to look in that book, he slid it aside and turned all of his attention to me.

"It must be really hard to have to deal with so much magick at once," he said. "Just try to relax. I'm right here. Nothing that's happened is too out of the ordinary."

"Everything is out of my ordinary," I moaned.

Instead of reading, we sat there for a while, talking. I found myself telling him about the dark wave and how frightened I had been. I told him about Hilary and all the things that had led up to my running away—all of the really personal things that I'd left out of my first explanation. I finally explained that I had a problem with telekinesis and that that what I was trying to find out more about.

"The newest thing," I explained, feeling my defenses collapse under the calming weight of his hand on my shoulder, "is that I can feel other witches around me. I can sense their feelings. I can sense my mother here, even though she's gone. I like the feeling of connection, but it also scares me. Everything comes so fast now. I'm never expecting any of it."

Then he leaned in, and his look took on a new level of seriousness.

"Can you feel my senses right now?" he said.

My body seemed to freeze in time. My heart stopped. I didn't breathe, didn't move. Everything was anticipation. I *could* feel him. He was going to ... what?

He came in close, took my face in one of his soft hands, and kissed me.

I'd never been kissed before, and I'd been kind of worried that I wouldn't know what to do when and if it ever happened. Luckily I didn't freak out or accidentally bite him or anything. I pressed into his mouth and responded naturally. He slipped his hands behind my neck and pulled me closer. Warmth . . . so much warmth. A universe of warmth. As he pulled away, he looked at me in happy surprise.

"I . . ." He seemed to catch himself speaking but didn't know what to say. "I've been wanting to do that since I saw you yesterday."

Could I speak? Did my mouth still work? Was my voice going to come out all funny? Only one way to find out.

"Me too," I said. "I mean, not kissing myself. You know. You."

Smooth, Soto. Smooth.

Fleeting concerns zapped through my brain. What about Brigid? What did this mean? Those feelings were numbed when I felt the sensation again. He wanted to pull me into him, and I wanted him to wrap his arms around me. But the flow cooled quickly, like we'd blown a fuse, and all the power went down. We must have become aware of it at the same moment. We sat very still and listened.

Someone was upstairs.

13

Attack

September 24, 1952

Goddess, Goddess, where have I been? I'm only just now getting the strength to get out of bed and resume my daily activities.

We opened the bith dearc two nights ago, Claire Findgoll and I, down on the shore below the house. It is a terrible yet fascinating thing, this small hole that rips through the fabric of the universe and seems to go on eternally. I maintained the dearc while Claire conducted the spell to try to draw Oona from the house into the opening. I am glad that Claire stood away from it, as it possesses a devastating force. It actually drains you of life energy. I feel as though I've been poisoned.

We haven't had any visitations since we performed the spell, but only time will tell if we've been successful.

Oh, I must go to sleep again. There is nothing left in me. No energy at all.

—Aoibheann

"Hello?" called a female voice. "Mom?"

"It's Brigid," Charlie whispered, all color draining from his face. "She's home early."

"Should I . . . hide down here while you go up?" I offered. Good one, Alisa. The sitcom solution always works so well in real life.

"No," he answered, shaking his head. "She knows we're here."

Brigid, I had figured, wasn't a powerful witch—but she was still a witch. Feeling another person's presence in the house seemed like something she would very well be able to do. We heard her walking through the kitchen and then opening the basement door.

"Okay," Charlie admitted, "this is kind of bad."

"What do we do?" I asked.

He squeezed my hand quickly, as a kind of apology for what was probably going to happen next. "I have no idea," he said.

"Hello?" Brigid called again. She approached the door to the library, which was still open behind us. "Aunt Evelyn?" Brigid said. She came down the steps and looked at the two of us, first in confusion and then with a growing flurry of emotion.

"Charlie? Alisa?" she said, her voice wavering. "What are you two doing here?"

"Researching," Charlie said simply.

"Researching?" she said. "You came in when we weren't here . . . *both* of you?"

Whether through magick or regular female intuition (which might also be magick, I don't know), Brigid seemed to know at once that there was a problem. She sat down on the bottom step, blocking our way out. Did kissing a witch leave a mark on your mouth? Did my lips glow? Could she see some kind of imprint?

"Alisa needed help," Charlie said. "She's trying to find out about her ancestors, and Evelyn definitely wasn't going to give her a hand. Sorry. We had to come in when Evelyn wasn't here."

"You could have told me," she said. "I would have helped you."

Oh. If we didn't feel bad before . . .

"So," she said, staring hard at me, "did you find anything?"

"A book," I said, immediately realizing how stupid that answer was. I went to a library and found . . . a book. Not for the first time in my life, I wished the floor would open under me and swallow me whole.

After a few moments of silence it finally dawned on me that I should leave them alone. I didn't want to leave Charlie to the wolves or anything, but I had no place here. They needed to talk. And I had a feeling Charlie was going to come clean about what had just occurred.

"I should probably go," I said, "before Evelyn gets home, like you said. She'd be furious to find me here."

"That might be a good idea." Charlie nodded. We probably realized at the same moment that he had driven me there.

"I'll walk back," I added. "I could use some fresh air." I tucked the book into my messenger bag. "I'll return this to Sam," I said to Brigid. "He'll put it back in the library." Then I did my walk of shame, crossing the room and heading to where she was perched.

Brigid slid aside to let me pass. She said nothing. She wouldn't—or couldn't—even look at me. As I stepped past, my leg brushed against her. I almost jumped as a surge went through that whole half of my body. I felt a wave of pure raw emotion coming off her. She might look furious, but inside, everything in her was weeping.

It was a long walk home through the mist and the wet, with my brain clanging around between elation and guilt.

I mean, *he* kissed *me*. What was I supposed to do? Slap him, like they do in old movies? Call him a cad? I hadn't done anything wrong.... It wasn't my fault....

But then I examined my motives. Did I want Charlie to kiss me? Yes. Had I kissed him back? Yes. Was he my cousin's boyfriend? Yes.

Guilty.

I sucked. I sucked, I sucked, I sucked.

But it still had been the best moment of my life. I had touched his face and felt the tiny, soft curls at the back of his head, down near his neck. It had been good, so good, too good. I still felt like I was walking through an incredible dream.

Yet Brigid's feelings were still so close, so strong. She loved Charlie—who wouldn't? He was adorable and funny and smart. Tall. Powerful. She had turned her back for a moment—to be responsible and go to work, no less—and then her weird new out-of-town cousin appeared, broke into her house, and made out with her boyfriend.

I trudged along, seagulls screaming overhead, my hair slowly collecting dampness from the air. It took me about forty-five minutes to get back to Sam's. When I got there, Enya was playing and delicious smells of garlic, fish, and cooking tomatoes were coming from the kitchen. Sam had obviously gone to the trouble to make sure I came back to a nice welcome—and I returned, the other woman, the coven wrecker. . . .

"Did you have a good day?" Sam asked, putting a salad bowl out on the table.

"Great!" I said, with forced enthusiasm.

"What did you do?"

"Oh," I said, picking up Mandu and letting him climb up on my shoulder, "just hung out with Charlie."

"Charlie's a great guy." Sam nodded. "A fantastic witch, too."

You have no idea, I thought. . . . Sam looked up at me strangely, and I banished all thoughts of Charlie from my mind and set a straight and steady expression on my face.

"Before I forget," he said, "I found some pictures of your mother I want to show you. Could you watch the stove for a second? And feel free to start the salad."

"Sure," I said, setting the cat on the floor. As Sam headed for the stairs, I started making the salad, dumping the mesclun into the salad bowl and replaying the kiss again and again in my mind. I set it against the music, felt the surge of bliss thrumming through my body. Charlie was so handsome, so tall, so funny, so nice, so smart, so . . .

Taken. By my cousin. What was I thinking?

I tossed some vinaigrette into the greens a little more aggressively than was really necessary. The cats cocked their heads at me.

Just as I had the night before, I suddenly felt something in the pit of my stomach telling me that something was wrong, very wrong. I looked up, all senses alert. Something was here. A presence. Something very foul. I let go of the salad tongs and looked around the kitchen.

And then it happened.

The first blow was on my left arm, and it sent me reeling backward, pain jagging all the way down into my hand. I heard glass shattering behind me. I whirled around to see all of the dishes flying out of the open rack under the cabinets, and they all came at me, one after the other. I didn't have time to move or to think. Something broke against my head. Glass fell onto my eyelids. I pulled up my arms to guard my face and head as best I could, but the blows were coming harder, pushing me back against the wall.

Something in me stirred, ready to do battle. I felt every fiber of my being tingling. I could stop this. I could . . .

I concentrated hard. Some of the dishes started to pop and splinter in midair, before they got to me. It was as if they were smashing against an invisible wall, and I knew I was doing it. No idea how—but I was doing it. Some still made it through. There were so many. The drawers were rattling, coming loose, coming at me. I dropped to the ground and started crawling for the table, elbowing my way through the shards.

I could see Sam trying to get to me, but I felt myself growing weak. Everything went to black and white, and there was a ringing in my ears that drowned out every other sound. I was fainting, I realized.

The next thing I knew, Sam was putting me down on the sofa. My clothes sparkled with bits of plate and drinking glass.

"I'm all glassy," I said, tears welling in my eyes. "Sam, I'm all glassy."

"I know," he said, checking over my head, my face, my eyes. "Look at me, Alisa. Look at me."

It was hard, but I focused on his face. He studied me.

"I'm going to take off my clothes," I said, standing uncertainly and wobbling from foot to foot. For some reason, the glass on my clothes was really preoccupying me. "I have to get this stuff away from me."

"Steady now, sweetheart." He looked over the shards that dangled like icicles from my clothes. He yanked a pair of pajamas from the top of my bag and set them down. "Get changed. I'll be back in a second."

I heard him run upstairs, heard the bang of a cabinet door. I pulled off my pants and T-shirt and dumped them in the center of the room. Then I put on some soothing fleece pants and the camisole pajama top. That was better. So much better.

I looked down and saw that my forearms were dripping blood.

The sofa loomed up at me, and I grabbed for it, holding tightly to the cushions for balance. And then everything went black again.

The lights in the room were dim. I was waking up. I was under a blanket. Was it morning? I didn't think so.

Where was I?

Sam's, I realized after a moment. The dishes. I remembered now. I looked up to see Ruth sitting next to me, holding an ice pack to my forehead with her uncasted arm. I tried to sit up, but she put a gentle hand on my shoulder.

"Stay down, Alisa," she said.

"What happened?" I asked.

"We don't know." Ruth smoothed my hair. "We're trying to figure it out."

"We?" I asked.

"Charlie was here when you were out," she said. "He put a ring of protection spells around the house."

"While I was out?"

"You've been unconscious for hours," she explained. "It's almost ten. Kate Giles is here now. She's another member of Ròiseal. She works in defensive magick."

"Where's Sam?" I asked, trying to lift my head to look around.

"Doing a divination spell to see if he can find out what caused this," she answered, indicating that I should rest again. "He's fine."

I took an inventory of myself. Both of my arms were wrapped in gauze from my palms to my elbows. I felt something on my head as well. I had no shirt on—that was probably why I was under the blanket. There were soft little things resting on various points of my stomach and chest—they felt like little cloth bags. I guessed they were full of herbs or witch ointments. I was generally a bit sore, but nothing felt broken.

I'd done a lot of strange telekinetic things in the last few weeks, but I'd never attacked myself. Also, what I'd felt right before the dishes started flying hadn't come from inside me. I'd felt something coming in from the outside, like a magickal draft. This time it hadn't been me. What was happening? I thought of calling Hunter. He would know what to do. This kind of thing was his job.

There was the sound of loud heels on the steps. A young woman, maybe just around Hilary's age, came into the room.

"She's awake," Ruth said. "Come on over."

The woman approached. She was striking—definitely shades of Raven. Her hair was long and auburn with a dramatic streak of blond in the front. She had a powerful body, with sleek, defined arms and a Celtic tattoo up near her right shoulder. The whole effect was set off by the form-fitting black pants, sleeveless shirt, and black boots she wore. This was Kate, I guessed. She looked really tough, but also feminine. Pretty much exactly how you think a female defensive magick expert should look—kick-ass and cool.

"Alisa, this is Kate," Ruth said, confirming my suspicion.

"Hi, Alisa," Kate said, sitting down on the floor next to me. "How do you feel?"

"Like I've just been hit on the head with a lot of plates."

She smiled. "Well, at least your sense of humor is still intact. That's a good sign." She looked up at Ruth. "Sam get anything?"

"Not yet." Ruth shook her head. "So, what do you think?"

"Well," Kate said, twisting one of her many silver rings, "it looks a little like Oona. I'm finding the same residual energy disturbance that I usually see after she graces us with her presence. It's not exactly the same, but it's close enough."

"But how can Oona be here?" Ruth asked, putting her hand to her head in concern.

"Beats me," Kate replied. "She's never transferred her energy like this before. This is totally new. Charlie covered this place well, but I'll add another layer of protection spells before I go. It's all I can think to do."

"Goddess," Ruth groaned, panic in her voice. "Oh, Goddess. It's spreading."

Sam came in from the kitchen. He looked to Kate, and she repeated what she had just said to Ruth. Then he came over to me.

"Hey, kiddo," he said, squatting down.

"Sorry about your dishes," I said.

He broke into a boyish grin and stroked my hair.

"Okay," Kate said, "I'd better get back. Don't worry, Alisa. We've been spelling this house for hours. Rest easy tonight. If you have any more trouble, Sam, I'm a phone call away."

Kate gave Ruth a gentle pat on the shoulder, pulled on a black leather jacket and a pair of gloves, and headed out.

"Do you want me to stay?" Ruth asked. "Or I'm sure Aunt Evelyn's home by now. We can call her . . ."

"No," Sam said, standing up. "Let's not. We've done all we can do. Alisa just has to be able to rest. There's nothing left here. I don't see any immediate threat."

She and Sam shared a long look, as if they were communicating telepathically. (Which they may have been able to do. I had no idea.) Ruth finally nodded.

"Leave these packs on for another half hour," she told Sam. "Also, put some marigold tisane and apple cider vinegar on a washcloth. You can apply that to the bruises tomorrow. But I'll check in and see how things are going."

After Ruth had gone, Sam and I sat down at the kitchen table and drank tea out of some paper cups he had left over from a picnic. Sam lent me a snuggly bathrobe to wear since I couldn't put my shirt back on over the packs that Ruth had attached to my chest with medical tape. The kitchen looked more or less normal, just with piles of broken glass swept into the corners.

"Tomorrow," he said, "I'm taking the day off. How about we go to Salem? You know, get out of here for a little while."

"Sounds great," I said, holding out a bandaged hand to accept a cookie he passed over to me from the counter. He looked like he wanted to say something but didn't quite know how to put it.

"What is it?" I asked, cracking the cookie in two.

"Some of those dishes," he said, his big blue eyes fixing on me hard. "I saw them burst in midair. They were being deflected."

"I have powers," I said quietly. Though there was nothing wrong with this fact, I treated it like it was my dirty secret. It still felt foreign.

"That's not possible," he answered, shaking his head.

"I don't know why or how, but I do," I said. "Honest."

"Goddess," he said. "So all this time, you've been fully capable of doing magick?"

"Yep," I said, biting my cookie. "Poorly, but I can."

Now that I thought of it, Sam would be the perfect person to teach me how to scry. Scrying seemed like a perfect way to get some information—maybe find out something about why I was supposed to come to Gloucester.

"You work in divination, right?" I said.

"Mostly," he replied.

"Can you teach me how to scry?"

"Scry?" He shrugged. "Sure. I can try. Not all witches can scry successfully. It's a personal thing, and there are lots of different methods. You have to find out which one is right for you. We'll try my method first. We're related, so we might use the same element."

He got up and went into the living room and returned with a large black bowl. He filled this from the contents of a jar he pulled from one of the kitchen cabinets.

"It's seawater," he said, setting the bowl down on the table. "I gather up a jar a week. A major rule of Wicca—never take more natural resources than you need, even from something as huge as the ocean."

Sam lectured me on the basics. I was impressed with the depth of his knowledge. Part of me always saw Sam as the goofy kid my mother had described in her book. Now I saw what he really was: a mature and incredibly responsible witch with years of training. He placed five white candles around the bowl, elevating them on stacks of books so that they sat just above the rim. After lighting them with a match, he turned off the overhead light.

"All right," he said, taking my hands. "Relax. Breathe deep. Focus on the water."

I did. At first nothing happened. It was just us, sitting in the dark, staring into a bowl of water for about twenty minutes. Then I realized that I was looking down through a square form, as if I was peering into a box. There was a flash of purple, then we were back to the water. I'd been hoping to see people, to hear them say clever, cryptic things. All I got was a box full of purple.

"I think I've had enough, Sam," I said, sighing.

"Did you see something?" he asked.

"I don't think it was anything," I said. "Just a flash of color."

"You're probably exhausted." He got up and turned on the light. "We'll try again when you're feeling better. For now, I think we both need some rest."

14

Witch Trials

March 21, 1953

Ostara already. I've been so busy the past few months, I've barely noticed how much time has gone by since the dearc. No visits from Oona, thank the Goddess. We seem to have been completely successful.

In the meantime the little child inside me grows and grows. She is a girl, of this I am certain. I never knew what utter joy motherhood would bring. I have become even more aware of the turning of the wheel and the phases of the moon. I feel her movement when the moon is full. She tends to be sleepy when it wanes.

—Aoibheann

Salem was only a short drive away, and Sam took a scenic route along the water. The sky was finally clear, and it was breezy. Aside from a few little aches and the cuts and bruises, I was fine. It was nice to get out alone with Sam.

Pulling into the town, I was amazed by all the Wiccans I

saw on the streets. Everyone seemed to have a pentacle necklace, or a tattoo, or something kind of witchy. In fact, the witch thing seemed to be done to death. Every store window seemed to feature a picture of a little figure in a black pointed hat, riding a broom. Sam parked in a lot near the visitors' center.

"Come on," he said. "There's something I want to show you."

Tucked behind some buildings next to the lot was an ancient cemetery, with thin, frail headstones—some sunk halfway into the ground. Next to this was a square sectioned off by a low stone wall. Heavy slabs of stone jutted out from the wall at equal intervals, forming benches.

"This is a weird park," I said as we entered the square.

"Have a better look," Sam told me, pointing to the first bench. I went over to it. There was writing there. It read: Bridget Bishop, Hanged, June 10, 1692. I continued around, looking at each bench. Sam followed along behind me. Sarah Wildes, hanged. Elizabeth Howe, hanged. Susannah Martin, Sarah Good, Rebecca Nurse, George Burroughs, Martha Carrier—all hanged. Giles Corey, pressed to death. There were more still, their names carved roughly into the stones. It was so stark, so disturbing.

"This is the Witch Trial Memorial," Sam explained. "These are the names of the people who were executed."

I knew a bit about the witch trials from school and from some reading I'd done on my own. Two young girls had made claims that they were bewitched. From there, accusations flew and a court was set up. People were dragged in to testify. The girls convulsed and seemed to go crazy. More people came forward, claiming that they too had been attacked. In the end, twenty people were executed and dozens more accused or affected. The whole thing was over in a few months; then the people who ran the court were forced to close it and apologize for what they'd done.

With a shiver I thought of my own behavior, how I'd wanted to write a letter to the local Widow's Vale paper and "expose" Wicca. While no one would have been tried or executed, I could have caused a lot of trouble for Morgan, Hunter, Mr. Niall . . . so many others. Thank God Mary K. and I hadn't actually done anything.

"You know what the weird thing is?" Sam said, looking down at the closest slab. "These people weren't witches at all. Some of them were outsiders, just a little weird in society's eyes. Some were prominent citizens. No rhyme or reason to it."

"Then what happened?" I asked. "Does anyone really understand?"

"Not really," he said, carefully brushing some dead leaves that obscured the name on the bench below us. "It was hysteria. People pointed to anyone in sight, claimed anything the judges asked them to claim—if only they would be allowed to live. People admitted to things they didn't do. If you didn't confess, they executed you. These people"—he indicated the benches around the square— "they wouldn't confess to things they hadn't done. They were very unlucky, and very brave."

"But now the town is full of witches," I said. "Why come here when the people who were killed weren't even Wiccans?"

"The idea still remains that witchcraft is evil and dark. I

guess we feel the need to come here and set the record straight."

"All this," I said, shivering as I looked over the bleak stone benches, "just because some girls made up stories about witches."

"It was more insidious than that," Sam said. "People were ready to rush to judgment, even to kill, just to exorcise their own dark thoughts and fears. Now everyone looks back on this, not understanding how it ever could have happened. But people still persecute and hurt one another over things they can't personally understand."

"I guess maybe you know something about that," I said.

He nodded, understanding my meaning. "I guess so. I've always been out as a witch, and I came out with my sexuality early as well. I refuse to lie."

"My mom never mentioned that you were gay. Did she know?"

"Well"—he exhaled and tucked his hands into the pockets of his jeans—"I came out when I was eighteen, a few years after your mother left. But she always knew. I could tell. She was incredibly empathetic. She probably didn't think it was a big deal; I guess that's why she didn't mention it."

My mother was empathetic. She could feel other people, sense their emotions—just like I had been doing more and more since I'd been here. I liked that part of being a witch. But the mention of my mother also brought my attention back to the graveyard with its decaying grave markers. We quietly walked away from the memorial.

"So," I said, "do you have a boyfriend, or . . . ?"

"I did," he said. "We separated about two months ago."

"Oh." I pushed some leaves around with my foot. "Sorry."

"Don't be," he said genuinely. "Shawn and I decided that we needed to be apart for a while."

"Shawn . . . was he a witch?" I asked.

"Yes." Sam nodded, staring out at the street. "He lives in Holyoke. It's nearby." He snapped back to his normal, sunny demeanor. "Okay," he said, "we're getting way too serious. Let me show you the cool stuff."

I followed Sam along, and he pointed out favorite restaurants, shops, and houses. We passed Bell, Book, and Candle—the shop where Charlie worked. We stepped in, but he wasn't there. I had to hide my profound disappointment. It wasn't like the blows to my head had given me amnesia. The incident in the library had been on my mind more or less nonstop from the moment I woke up. I wondered what had happened between Charlie and Brigid. It couldn't have been good. Maybe, I thought, cringing with guilt—maybe he was breaking up with her at this very moment. Maybe that's why he wasn't at work.

Not likely.

Uggggh. Too much to think about. I still felt guilty. Maybe it was a good thing the plates had knocked me senseless last night. I probably would be a basket case otherwise.

After picking up a birthday gift for Ruth, Sam took me to an old hotel for lunch. He told me stories about my mother, all kinds of brother-sister high jinks. As we were talking and enjoying ourselves, I realized how good Sam was being to me. He'd put me up and cared for me with no advance warning at all. He'd stood up to his family to defend me. I owed him my honesty. There was a convenient lull in the conversation as Sam was eating. I decided to use it.

"My dad doesn't know where I am," I said, not looking up. "I ran away."

Sam stopped eating, set down his fork, and waited for me to continue. He didn't look all that surprised. With that stunning introduction, I proceeded to tell him the whole story— and I mean the *whole* story. Everything from the dark wave to Hilary to the night I ran away. The entire Alisa Soto soap opera.

"I've been calling someone from my coven," I said, coming to the end. "She put a watch sigil on me so that she'd be able to find me if I wasn't in touch."

"That's something, I guess," he said, processing the information for a moment. Then he dug into the pocket of his brown suede jacket, pulled out a tiny cell phone, and plunked it down on the table.

I got the hint.

When the first sound I heard was Hilary's voice, I readied myself to snap the phone closed again but then thought better of it. Sam was trusting me to call my family—and Hilary, like it or not, was family now.

"Hi, Hilary," I said, trying to sound cheerful, as if this was the most normal call in the world.

"Alisa? Is that you?" She sounded breathy, really alarmed.

"It's me. Hi."

"Where are you?"

"Safe," I said firmly. "Fine. Staying in a nice warm house, eating three meals a day. Nothing to worry about."

"Nothing to worry about? Alisa, your father's about to

have a heart attack, and . . ." I heard her stop and steady herself. She must have known I could be spooked away.

"I just called to tell you guys that I was okay," I said. "That's all. Is Dad around?"

"No, he's at work, sweet— Alisa."

She caught herself so abruptly, I actually felt bad, like I'd been way too rough on her. I knew she wasn't all bad.

"How are you feeling?" I asked.

"How am *I* feeling?" She was surprised. "Oh, I'm fine. Good. A little jumpy the last few days."

We actually made some small talk over the next few minutes. I think I was even able to convince her that I really was fine. I didn't sound crazy or strung out. In fact, I was about a million times calmer than I usually was at home. She told me that they'd stopped doing any planning or moving during the time I'd been gone, but that she'd had an ultrasound done. I was going to have a little brother. This news didn't nauseate me as much I would have imagined, and I even congratulated her with some real excitement. As I said good-bye, I felt like a changed woman. She would probably recommend to my dad that I be allowed to run away more often.

I'd asked Sam if I could make one more quick call, and he'd agreed. I dialed Hunter's number.

Hunter, I noticed, sounded even more adult and more British on the phone. His voice was deeper, and I could almost feel him pacing.

"Alisa!" he said, exhaling loudly.

I filled him in on the situation so far, and he hmm-ed and ah-ed in typical Hunter fashion. He'd gotten most of the story from Morgan, so I didn't have to start from the very beginning.

"Have you spoken to your father?" he asked, with just a slightly parental edge to his voice. "Morgan tells me he's very upset, understandably."

"I just spoke to Hilary for a few minutes," I said. "Everything's fine."

"Well," he said, clearly not sure if he believed that last statement of mine, "I have some news as well, and it fits in rather neatly with what you've just told me. I spoke to both Ardán Rourke and Jon Vorwald. Jon said that it's possible that you have a trigger element, but he'll have to test you in person to figure out what that might be. He also said that he'd heard of one case, back in the fifties, of a telekinetic power that seemed to be passed down via firstborn female children."

"Firstborn females?" I frowned. Actually, that would explain why my mother and I had telekinesis, but not Sam or Ruth. But if it was passed down to my mother . . . then Evelyn . . .

"That's right." Hunter's crisp voice interrupted my thoughts. "Also, and this is very interesting, Ardán knew of at least one case of a witch in the 1800s who had telekinesis. What's interesting about her is that when she got older, maybe sixty or seventy, her telekinetic incidents became more violent, harder to control. He thinks that it's possible that as witches get older, they lose some of their inhibitions. Their emotions become stronger and harder to rein in."

"I don't understand," I said. "What does that have to do with me? I'm fifteen."

"Think about it," he said. "You have telekinesis. Your mother had it. It's quite possible, then, that your *grandmother* has it. You just said that the incidents were getting worse with time and that they also flared up during times of family crisis."

Evelyn. I sucked in my breath. This could be Evelyn. It made complete sense—to me, anyway. When Evelyn was upset or under stress, that was when Oona was at her worst. But what could I do with this information? If she didn't already hate me, Evelyn would really lose it if I came forward and suggested that she was responsible for all of the horrible things that had happened to her family. Besides that, I didn't have enough proof to be sure that it was true.

"Hello?" Hunter drew me back to reality. "Alisa?"

"Still here," I said, gripping the lobby wall. "God, Hunter. What do I do now?"

"I wouldn't do anything yet. We can't be sure that this is actually what's going on. It's just a theory. Ardán's looking into the matter some more. Your case really interested him, and he wants to come over and meet you."

"What can I say?" I said. "I'm fascinating."

"So," he said, "when can we expect to see you?"

"Uh . . ." I shifted from foot to foot. "Soon. I promise. Spring break is almost over. I just need a little more time."

In the end, I had to promise to call him the next night, after the Ròiseal circle. Reeling from what I'd just heard, I headed back into the dining room. Should I tell Sam? No. Hunter had said to wait until he had more information. Waiting. Not my strong suit.

As I came into the dining room, the waitress approached our table with the biggest brownie sundae I had ever seen.

I sighed. Sam was *the best.*

15

Ròiseal

february 3, 1955

The baby will be coming any day now. At the Imbolc celebration last night, all of Ròiseal performed a ritual to ensure a safe birth.

Just as I knew Sorcha was a girl, I know this is a boy — a rascally little boy, at that. from the way he kicks, I tend to think that he will give his sister no peace! He's feisty! We have decided to name him Somhairle.

Sorcha seems to know that something is going on. I can tell by the look in her eye. She likes to run up and touch my stomach, then she giggles and runs away. She'll sometimes drag Hugh over and point it out to him, her eyes full of wonder. My little girl — she's so full of the Goddess!

— Aoibheann

"Looks like we're the last ones here," Sam said as we parked between Charlie's Volkswagen and a red motorcycle.

Just the sight of Charlie's car turned me into jellyfish woman, with wobbly legs and a googly stare, but I managed to pull myself together enough to be able to walk to the front door like a normal human.

Sam let us right in and headed for the living room, where everyone was already gathered. A fire was going strong in the fireplace. In the middle of the room there was a cauldron filled with cool water and flower blossoms. Ruth's birthday cake was set on a small table, uncut.

It wasn't exactly a rocking party. Brigid, Ruth, and Evelyn sat together on a long sofa, all looking uncomfortable. Ruth's heavy cast was obviously itching. Brigid looked tired and pensive. Evelyn was her usual sparkling self. The three of them were having a quiet conversation with Kate Giles. Ruth and Kate each gave me a hug when they saw me. Brigid and Evelyn each gave me a thousand-yard stare.

After giving Ruth her gift, Sam settled down across the room, where Charlie was sitting with an older man. I tried to look as casual as possible as I joined him there—my mind, however, was constantly replaying our kiss. I had the DVD version going, with multiple angles, the trailer with the highlights, and the full director's cut. Charlie eyed the bruise near my eye, and I nodded to indicate that I really was all right.

The man next to Charlie was dressed kind of formally in a neat gray suit with a light cream-colored sweater underneath the jacket. He was just as tall, but heavier. He looked like Charlie, with the same kind face and the mischievous peaked eyebrows, and though his hair was shot through with silver gray, it curled defiantly. I knew instantly that this was Charlie's father.

"You're Alisa!" the man boomed, looking straight at me. He spoke so loudly that it startled some of the others. No drawn-out introductions needed here. Everyone should have a weird witch vibe. It makes things so much easier.

"My dad," Charlie said.

"I understand you were raised by nonwitches, Alisa! I'd love to know what that was like," his dad added. Charlie's eyes went wide, then rolled back into his head in comic grief.

"My dad," Charlie repeated, containing an exasperated sigh. "Right to the point."

"Did I say something wrong?" his father asked innocently. From Charlie's description of his father, I could easily see that he might have some strange people skills.

"It's okay." I laughed. "If you have a few days to spare, I can tell you the whole story."

"I'm not sure if I have a few entire days," he said, sipping his tea and honestly thinking it over, "but I'll check my schedule. Perhaps we can do a few blocks of time over the course of a week."

Okay. He was very literal, too, but he seemed nice enough. I couldn't imagine Charlie coming from a family that wasn't nice.

"I was just going to get something to drink," Charlie said, standing up. "Would anyone like anything?"

He ended up getting orders from almost everyone in the room, so I immediately sprang up and offered to help, praying that I didn't look too obvious and scheming. However, I did notice Brigid slipping me a steely glare as I left.

I followed Charlie into the kitchen. He was at the counter, setting down the glasses. He looked so good, just simply dressed in a dark blue button-down shirt and jeans. He seemed extra tall, so much more adult looking than me. There was no way I could have kissed him. I must have been delusional.

"Hi," I finally said. That was the best I could do. Words were failing me.

"Hey," he said, giving me a little smile—not his usual light-up-the-room beam. "How are you? Are you okay?" I thought I saw his hand moving, as if he was going to reach out to me, but he pulled it back and moved the glasses around instead.

"I'm fine." I nodded. "Thanks for coming last night. I felt a lot safer knowing that you protected the house. Sorry I was, um . . . unconscious."

"Don't worry about it," he said. "I guess it was that whole getting-hit-on-the-head-with-everything-in-the-kitchen thing."

"Something like that," I agreed.

I could see the coppery freckles under his eyes in the warm glow of the kitchen light. I felt warmth coming from him but also something else—pain, maybe. Definitely stress. It made me want to . . . I don't know, give him a big hug or something. He wasn't himself.

"Maybe we could talk?" I said.

"This isn't really a good time," he said, opening the refrigerator and pulling out some drinks. His smooth brow furrowed, as if he really, really had to concentrate on sorting out the beverages.

"Is everything okay?" I asked.

"Everything's fine."

That wasn't true. I could see that. "You're not supposed to lie to witches," I said. "Remember? You're not even supposed to tell half-truths to half witches."

"Right." He sighed, putting the drinks on the counter and leaning against the refrigerator. "Good point. Sorry."

"So," I said, "what's up?"

"Look," he said, as if he was searching for the words, "I can't talk right now."

"Okay," I said uncertainly. "Do you want to give me a call later?"

"I'm going to be busy tonight." He sighed again. "Maybe tomorrow, okay?"

With Brigid. That's what he wasn't saying. He was going to be talking to Brigid. His girlfriend. The person he was supposed to be talking to.

"Oh, sure," I said. Though I tried to keep smiling, I felt my face fall. I was rapidly coming to my senses. Why had I followed him? What had I been expecting him to say? Did I think he was going to jump up and down with joy and tell me that he'd ditched Brigid? At best, our kiss caused major problems. At worst, he was regretting that he'd ever met me. Although who could say? Maybe there was something even worse than that.

I turned and started filling the glasses quickly.

"Alisa . . ." he said. Again I saw his hand moving, as if he wanted take hold of me. Again he held himself back. There was a rush of frustration coming from him.

"It's okay," I told him, fixing the limp smile back on my face. "Tomorrow or whenever you have a chance. Just give me a call."

I saw that he was about to reply, but I scooped up some of the glasses and headed out. One more word and I knew I would be bawling. I couldn't risk it.

Back in the living room, I passed around the drinks and sat down next to Sam, who gave me a strange look. I knew he must have realized I was upset about something, but he probably assumed that it was related to Evelyn. He inched closer to me, and I felt a little better having him by my side. Charlie followed a moment later and gave out the other cups.

"It's a little chilly in here," Ruth observed, pulling her sweater around her uncasted arm.

Since Charlie was next to the fireplace, he reached down to put another log on the fire. I was sitting next to the fireplace, and he glanced up and caught my eye for a moment. I couldn't meet his gaze, so I threw my attention across the room. Of course, I looked right up at Evelyn. She was staring at me. The room *was* cold. Very cold. And the force of her stare made me even colder.

Suddenly Ruth screamed, and I felt a rush of extreme heat cutting the chill. As if it had been stirred by some unnatural breeze, the fire in the fireplace leaped out, blue with heat. It reached for Charlie, licking at his clothes, his skin. I felt a fear rising up through me. Charlie was going to be hurt—badly.

No. I could not let this happen.

Water . . . I thought, my body standing itself up and my hand raising without my willing either to do so. I pointed at the caldron, and it lifted itself from its resting place. Time was slow now—I was unaffected by it. The water would do what I needed it to do; I had only to ask it. Once again words came to me from the recesses of my mind, in an echo of a woman's voice, a voice I couldn't quite place.

"*Cuir as a srad,*" I said, moving my pointed finger to indicate Charlie. "*Doirt air.*"

The caldron sailed through the room, past Charlie, and smashed itself against the smoky brick of the fireplace, spilling all of the flowers and water onto him. He stumbled back as it thundered to the floor and rolled back and forth before the fire.

The crash brought me back in step with everything else, and I lurched forward, as if I was in a car that had skidded to a halt. Charlie quickly rolled away from the fireplace and looked down at himself in shock. He was soaking wet and covered in soggy flower pieces. His hands were singed, but the water had protected him somewhat, keeping his clothing from igniting.

"I'm okay," he said, patting his body down and checking for injuries. "I'm okay." Brigid and Ruth descended on him, dragging him off to the kitchen to attend to the burns. The whole thing had happened in less than a minute.

"Goddess," said Kate once they had gone, "did everyone just see that?"

I became aware of the fact that everyone left in the room was staring at me. My hand was still outstretched. I jammed it behind my back.

Charlie's father was next to me. All traces of cosmic goofiness were gone from his face.

"Thank you," he said, reaching out to squeeze my arm. His face was pale with shock. "I've never seen anyone do a deflection that quickly before."

"You're welcome," I mumbled. "I mean . . . I just did it."

Sometimes I just blow myself away with my fancy talk.

"You do know," he said seriously, "that you moved the

cauldron almost *simultaneously* with the flame, killing its progress—don't you?"

"I did?" I said, feeling very dull-witted.

"You gave a command spell," Charlie's father said. "Very simple. The energy was channeled through the water. The Gaelic charge was basic. But it was very, very fast, and you brought up a lot of energy within a moment."

I wobbled, and Sam gently helped me to sit down. Evelyn, I noticed, had returned and was looking at me up, down, and sideways.

"You have powers," she said.

She didn't sound happy, or amazed, or impressed, or grateful. She sounded suspicious.

"She not only has powers," Charlie's father added, "she's strong. Quite strong. And fast. And she has a rather shocking command of spell language."

"Have you been studying with someone?" Kate asked, pulling up an ottoman and sitting close to me.

"A Seeker," I said, looking around nervously.

"A Seeker?" she said. "Goddess. For how long?"

"A few weeks. On and off over the last few months."

"A few *weeks*?" she repeated after me again. "That's it?"

"So," Evelyn said, "you have powers—somehow—and you've been studying with someone from the council."

Evelyn hadn't exactly been sending valentines to the council. I realized that I'd just made another huge mistake in her eyes.

"He's from the council," I said, trying to defend myself, "but he's not teaching me as a representative of the council. I mean, he's just my coven leader...."

Ruth looked in through the doorway.

"Charlie's fine," she said. "The burns on his hands are minor. I treated him with some aloe. We'll add a preparation of calendula and cantharis. Brigid is mixing it up now."

There was a murmur of relief from everyone. I felt like I needed air. I was on emotional overdrive. I tugged on Sam's sleeve, hoping he would understand the can-we-go message. Fortunately, Sam is perceptive.

"I think," he said, standing and pulling his keys from his pocket, "that we should call it a night. Alisa's still kind of worn out from last night, and this has been a long day."

I nodded in confirmation. It was an awkward and hasty exit, but then, this was the House of Strange Happenings. Sam said nothing—just took me home and let me spend some time with my thoughts. I certainly had enough of those.

After Sam had gone to bed, I found that I was still wide awake. I stared at the phone for a while, trying to will it to ring. I thought about calling Charlie, even though he'd indicated pretty clearly that he didn't want to talk to me tonight. Bad idea.

I was going to go crazy if I didn't think of something to do.

First I tried scrying again, but I was even less successful than I'd been the night before. Giving that up, I went for my bag and pulled out Máirín's book. I set it down next to the scrying bowl and started to read. As I did so, Astrophe jumped into my lap, causing me to flinch. My elbow struck the bowl, causing it to splash water on the pages.

The ink began to run. I almost screamed.

I scrambled around, grabbing for paper towels, anything to blot the water. I couldn't find anything. Everything must have been used up in the cleanup the night before. Frantic, I ran back to the book to try to brush the water from the page with my hands, only to make an amazing discovery: Something was there that hadn't been there before.

It came into clearer focus as the water ran out over it. There was writing there, scribbled all over the margins, squeezed into every available inch of space. There were combinations of runes, symbols, bits of Gaelic, and words in English—*uncontrollable magick—Rowanwand—stabilization of energies, provided that the* . . .

The water was bringing it out. If I wanted to fill out the passages, my only choice would be to drip on more. Using a spoon, I tried this very carefully, working drop by drop. By doing this, one passage became clear enough to read:

. . . *this plague of uncontrollable magick, the roots of which are all too human, forged by the dark spell of our poor tortured ancestor. Being Rowanwand, we pride ourselves on our ability to master knowledge and control our destiny. Pride, of course, is well known to be one of the deadliest vices. Fear is another. Both were at work when I destroyed the pages in a fit of terrified rage. I was fifteen years old at the time. I hope now to rectify my mistakes and to add to our store of knowledge. . . .*

It went into the Gaelic and symbols. I saw the occasional word in English here or there, but no passage was entirely clear, and I was worried about actually destroying the book in my attempts to extract the information.

Even though I felt guilty about making a long-distance call without asking Sam first, I knew I had to tell someone about this right away. This was *huge*. Besides, it was after nine. The rates were cheaper. I called Hunter. Much to my irritation, though, he wasn't home, and neither was his father. I left a garbled message for him, frantically trying to explain what I had seen.

Now what? I knew that this was important. Someone had to see this. Maybe even . . . Evelyn?

Sam kept a bike on the side of the house. If I used that, I could be to Evelyn's and back in no time. The hills would be a pain going up, but I'd get back really quickly. Since this seemed to be my big week for impulsive behavior, I decided to go for it. Compared to what I'd done so far, taking a bike for a midnight ride was nothing. I put the book into my messenger bag and let myself out.

The town was beautiful at night. I rode along the water. There was plenty of light from the ships and reflections of the moon on the harbor. The breeze was moist and heavy, cold but not biting. I couldn't help but notice that the view looked a lot like my last dream, with the dark, calm sea and the waxing moon hanging in the sky. Of course, there was no mermaid.

The last hill up to Evelyn's was horrible—I would feel it in the morning—but I needed the exercise, anyway. The house was completely dark. I walked the bike up to the porch, looking above me for falling branches or tiles or posts. I carefully put the book between the screen and the door and hurried back to the bike and rode away, trying to get back as quickly as possible.

I woke up at eight in the morning to the sound of the phone ringing. Sam called down from his room to tell me that the call was for me. There was a strange note in his voice. Cautiously I picked up the phone.

"Alisa."

It was Evelyn. Yikes.

"Yes?

"I want to talk to you. This morning. Can you be here at ten?"

"Sure," I said, quaking.

"Fine. Good-bye."

And that was that. I was left staring at the phone.

16

Bloodline

October 3, 1971

There was an incident today in the kitchen.

Sorcha came to me, extremely upset. She was speaking wildly about the craft, saying that it was dangerous and that we shouldn't be allowed to wield as much power as we do. I attributed the remarks to an emotional reaction to the storm. Both Somhairle and Sorcha seem to have been very affected by it.

As we were speaking, one of the drawers pulled itself out and flew across the room, right at Sorcha. She stepped aside, and it fell to the ground. In the same moment, the cabinets started to open up and the dishes came at us. We had to throw ourselves to the ground.

This can mean only one thing — Oona has returned.

I have already called Claire Findgoll and Patience Stamp. They are coming to help me cast spells of protection this afternoon. Patience has no one to watch her little daughter Kate, so I will be able to distract Somhairle and Sorcha with babysitting. My mind *is racing, though. Will I be forced to reopen the dearc? And how is it possible that Oona would come back after so long, and why after this horrible storm?*

I have a terrible feeling in the pit of my stomach.

—Aoibheann

Sam was quiet as he drove me to Evelyn's. I could see that he was baffled by this sudden morning visit, and my brain was too addled for me to be able to explain. Evelyn met me at the door and took me directly to her study without saying a word. She indicated that I should sit.

"You left something very interesting for me to read," she said. "We need to discuss it."

I nodded stiffly. I wasn't even going to ask how she knew it was me. She crossed around to her desk and carefully picked up Máirín's Book of Shadows and her athame. She ran the athame over the cover and the spine of the book, and it took on a faint phosphorescent quality.

"I've examined this closely through the morning," she said, turning it over in her hands, covering every inch with the athame. "I see that there are quite a number of spells on this book. One of them is an attraction spell, designed to help those of us looking for an answer to our family difficulty find it. I'm sure it helped you. Where was it?"

"In your library," I said sheepishly. She didn't seem surprised that I'd been there, even though it meant that I'd broken into her house and snooped around. She nodded thoughtfully.

"Was it hidden?" she asked.

"Well"—I shook my head—"sort of. It was misfiled and

mislabeled. That's all." I looked at the spine. The German writing was gone. "It had German on the spine," I said, confused. "It would appear and disappear."

That didn't seem to surprise her, either. "There are quite a few glamors on this book," she said. I was waiting for her to start explaining the green writing, but she kept examining the cover, as if it was the most interesting thing imaginable.

"I found this book when I was a girl," she said, a trace of a strange smile appearing on her thin lips. "It vanished from my room before I had a chance to look it over thoroughly."

"What happened?" I asked.

"In all likelihood," she said, "my mother took it. She could see how agitated it had made me, so she decided it was best for me not to read it. But aside from Oona's story, which is very tragic, there's nothing in here worth hiding. The fact that someone has torn out some of the pages, however, suggests a very serious problem. No Rowanwand destroys a book—especially not the Book of Shadows of an ancestor."

"Who do you think tore out the pages?" I said.

"I don't know," Evelyn replied. "The pages were torn when I located the book. It seems to be the same witch who wrote the spell in secret writing, but I don't know her identity. I see that the ink is smudged now. It wasn't when I first found it. Someone else was trying to make the book unreadable."

"No." I shook my head. "That was me, and it was an accident. Couldn't you see it?"

Her eyes narrowed in on me.

"See what?" she asked.

"The writing," I said. "The green writing."

She looked like I'd just given her a shock of static electricity.

"What green writing?"

I got up and took the book from her, quickly flipping through the pages.

"It's gone," I said, speeding through. "It was here, and now it's gone."

She looked at me, demanding further explanation, and I told her about the water spilling onto the book and the mysterious writing that blossomed like creeping vines all over the page.

"I saw it," I promised her. "It's gone now."

"The spell could be old," she said, her eyes flashing. "It could be fragile. Or the spells may be counteracting one another. That could account for the fading. I'd say we should try dampening it again, but we might destroy it."

"That's what I was afraid of." I nodded.

"Did you get a good look at the pages?" she asked.

"Pretty good. But I didn't understand all of the words. Some of them were written in another language."

"Then I have an idea. Have you ever heard of a ritual called a *tàth meànma*?"

"I've done one of those," I said. "I did a *tàth meànma brach*."

Evelyn looked up at me with knitted brows.

"Somehow I doubt that," she said. From Charlie's reaction, I knew that this probably did seem unlikely. But I guessed she would find out that I was telling the truth soon enough. "It's a very intense connection spell that can only be performed by . . ."

"I know what it is," I said, starting to feel a little annoyed. "I did one."

She looked a bit surprised, but she seemed to like the fact that I showed I actually had bits and pieces of spine every once in a while.

"All right," she replied, still skeptical, "how do you feel about doing a regular *tàth meànma* so that I can have a look at the pages?"

The idea of having Evelyn in my mind was more than a little scary, but I knew this was the only way we were going to get to the bottom of the story.

"Okay," I said.

Evelyn instructed me to sit down and meditate for a few minutes while she prepared some ritual tea. I sat cross-legged on the floor and did some breathing exercises that we'd been taught in circle. I would show her. *Tàth meànma* . . . bring it on!

She returned for me a few minutes later and indicated that I should come to the kitchen. I got up and followed her.

"Drink it all," she said, pointing at a huge cup of tea.

This stuff was nasty. Seriously nasty. It tasted like I was licking a slimy, insect-infested tree. But I gulped it back, determined to show no signs of weakness. She drank one herself, and I saw her grimace slightly. When we had gotten this down, we sat cross-legged on the polished wood floor, took each other's hands, and put our foreheads together.

"Relax," she said. "Just breathe."

At first I just felt my butt getting sore and heard the hum of the refrigerator.

I became gradually aware that I wasn't in the kitchen

anymore. I wasn't sure where we were. It might have been on the shore because I thought I could hear the sound of the ocean. The ground was soft, like cool, damp sand.

"Come, Alisa." Evelyn's voice was somewhere in my mind—not in sound. I could feel the words. I started walking along, not sure where to go. Then I saw that Evelyn was beside me. I could tell that she was somehow in control of the experience, that she was the guide.

What came next was a weird mix of images—a falling piece of furniture, the sound of splintering wood and ripping fabric. A storm. A baby. Evelyn—or both of us—was holding a baby. Sorcha was her name—Sorcha . . . Sarah . . . my mother. Evelyn led me away from this image. There was an overwhelming love of the Goddess. I could feel her power all around me, especially in the ocean. And I felt walls— anger, sadness, terrible loss—a father, a mother, a sister named Tioma, also named Jessica, killed in a car accident, a husband dying quietly in his sleep, a daughter gone forever . . . unbearable sadness . . .

We were leaving Evelyn, and Evelyn was coming into me. Evelyn drank up my life, taking in everything. She saw me, at three years old, trying to understand my father's explanation that my mother was gone and that she was never coming back. She saw my life in Texas—the long flatness of the land and the constant warmth of the sun. Then New York State, Widow's Vale, so cold and bleak and lonely.

I felt her close attention to the whirlwind of events that followed—discovering Wicca, my fears at seeing what magick could do, my hospitalization. Finding my mother's Book of Shadows and realizing I was a blood witch. As we came to the point where I was standing alone as the dark wave approached, linked to Morgan through the *brach*, I felt her speeding, falling through my mind. This she couldn't take in enough of, and she could hardly believe what she was seeing. She couldn't get to everything I had learned through Morgan, but the power she saw there was unlike anything she had ever encountered. She saw me finish the spell as the dark wave closed in, and I felt her pride.

There was an interested pause as she caught a flash of my strange dreams about Gloucester and the mermaid. I felt her mind hooking onto the images and processing them in some way. And I was *telekinetic?* Sparks of surprise as she saw objects falling, flying, breaking . . .

After that, her emotions changed, softened. I came to something raw within her. She felt for me as I returned to the house where no one understood what I had seen or been through. She was with me on the floor at Hunter's as I wept, full of frustration and pain. Then she saw me running away, coming to her, and how rejected I felt. Her guilt was thick, smothering. Images of my mother flickered through our minds.

She was moving faster now, through the events of the last few days. We came to Charlie—my ripple of excitement at meeting him, our kiss in the library. I cringed—how embarrassing!

The book. That was what she wanted to see. Finally we faced the book with its strange green print. She pulled in close to it and read the pages. What was odd was that now I could see even more writing that had been invisible before, along with the passages I had been able to uncover. Telekinesis . . . she was thinking again . . . uncontrollable magick

. . . uncontrollable . . . The word was making her uncomfortable.

Then she saw what I had concluded—what I had asked Hunter to look into—what Ardán Rourke had suggested . . . that she also suffered from telekinesis. There was no ghost. No Oona. No . . .

Everything was rushing back at me, a rush of gravity, pressing on my head, making my stomach churn. I wanted to get up—to move around, to stretch and feel the blood flowing through my veins. But she put a hand on my shoulder.

"Sit," she said. "It catches up with you."

I sat. It caught up with me. I wondered if I was going to barf.

"You," she said, "you're telekinetic?"

I nodded and steadied myself.

"And the Seeker is trying to find out if it is hereditary?"

I nodded again. "He thinks it may be passed down by firstborn females. Like my mother, me . . . and you." I looked at Evelyn. "Think about it," I said softly. "When did you have the most problems with Oona? When something bad happened? When you were upset or confused? That's when it happens to me."

No answer. She stared at some tiny birds that had come to eat at a bird feeder outside her window.

"What you saw in the book," Evelyn said, "I understood what it was saying. The passage suggests that Oona performed a spell—probably a bit of dark magick. The result brought telekinesis into our family, starting with Máirín."

"What else did it say?" I asked, my voice hoarse.

"There is no cure—at least, not that the writer knows of. The attacks are caused by repressing emotions, so the only solution is to try not to bottle them up. The more they are kept under pressure, the greater the explosions."

"What about the missing pages?"

"The spellwriter admits to ripping out any pages relating to a description of telekinesis. Later in life she regretted it. She spent many years investigating the problem, with only some success."

"But why did she destroy them?" I asked, shaking my head. "I don't get it."

"All good witches pride themselves on control." Evelyn sighed. "Rowanwands especially. We rely on the power that our knowledge gives us and the control we have over it. When a witch's control is in question, his or her power may be reined in. Most of us will do anything to avoid that fate, even lie when we are ill or weak. The woman who wrote these words was smart enough to know that if her own fear and pride could actually cause her to tear out pages in a book that described a family affliction, there was a good chance that one of her descendants might do the same. So she hid her writing and spelled the book so that it could be found by the right people—people ready to face the truth, to admit that they didn't have the control that they thought they had."

She leaned her back against the refrigerator, legs akimbo, looking more like a stunned teenager than the imposing, matronly woman I had known. "That's why I couldn't see this book for years," she added. "I was open to ideas the first time I found it. When my mind closed up, the book became invisible to me. All these years . . ." She shook her head as realization lit her eyes. "I could have done something about these problems. Oh, Goddess, Sorcha . . ."

Suddenly Evelyn's composure completely abandoned her, and her face crumpled into a sob. "Sarah, your mother," she whimpered as her age finally seemed to show, "she had it, too. She stripped herself because she was frightened by her powers. Her telekinesis." Evelyn closed her eyes and sobbed again. "Oh, Goddess, I could have saved her. . . ."

I shook my head, reaching out to take her hand. "You didn't know," I said.

"I should have," she whispered. "It was all there for me to put together. If I had been honest with her, if I had told her about what was happening to me instead of just pushing her away . . ."

"You couldn't have known what she was planning," I said, squeezing her hand. "She was frightened, and she didn't tell you how deep her fears went."

Evelyn sighed wearily. "I could see how frightened she was. I thought I could take care of Oona on my own." She looked me in the eye. "I pushed my daughter away," she concluded, wiping her eyes with the back of her hand. "And I lost her."

She looked over at me, slowly regaining her composure. I opened my mouth to say something, but nothing came out. I was suddenly profoundly aware that I could pass on telekinesis to *my* daughter, if I ever had one. Looking at Evelyn's tearstained face, I swore to myself that I would always be honest with my children. And open.

"I'll have to tell them the truth," she said, sitting up straight again. "There is no Oona."

"No," I said. "You were right. She was real, and she cast the spell that's affecting us."

"I suppose," she replied. "All these years, I thought it was something entirely outside myself, something I could eventually control. But it was coming through me. It was always me."

I could tell it was more than she could bear.

"The Seeker," she said, "he's working with a chaos specialist in London to find a remedy?"

"A chaos specialist?"

"That's what someone who specializes in uncontrollable magick is called." She smiled wryly.

"Yes," I answered, slightly chilled by the term *chaos specialist*. That had a really bad sound to it. Hunter had obviously been trying to be delicate. "He is."

"Well, then," she said. "I suppose we'll have to see what he comes up with." She pulled herself off the floor, moving stiffly.

"I'm not going to tell anyone up here about this," I said as I watched her. "I'm only going to tell some people in my coven and that man Ardán. This can just be between us. We'll tell them that we found something to bring Oona partially under control."

Evelyn's eyes looked pale and red rimmed in the sunlight from the window. She turned to me. For the first time I felt something coming from her, something warm.

"Thank you," she said simply.

"I should go," I said, gathering up my things. "I mean . . . I should rest before the circle."

Evelyn nodded and put her hand on my shoulder as she walked me to the front door. "Have a good rest, Alisa. And thank you." She looked me in the eye. "I am very lucky that you chose to visit."

"You're welcome," I whispered, and walked slowly down the front steps and along the roads to Sam's house. I wasn't very tired. I just thought Evelyn needed some time alone. She'd just learned some serious things about my mother and her leaving, and I knew it would take her a long time to come to terms with them.

If she ever did.

17

The Mermaid

November 14, 1971

Sorcha has been gone for one month. Hugh and I have decided that we will not scry for her anymore. She is gone.

Somhairle raged when we told him of our decision. He screamed. He threatened to leave as well, to go and find her himself. Then he stormed out of the house to walk off some of his anger. Soon, I think, his emotions will regulate themselves and he will understand. Sorcha has willingly given up her power. She has refused the blessing of the Goddess and turned her back on her heritage. When a witch is stripped, it is understood: No longer shall that witch be one of us. Sorcha made it easier for everyone by taking herself away.

While I know what I must do, and while I know I am right, my heart is broken. I feel hollow, as if a hole has been drilled in me and all feeling has gone forever. Hugh looks gray, and I worry about his health. This has taken a great toll on him.

After Somhairle left, we heard a noise upstairs in Sorcha's room. We found her quilt in shreds, her books on the ground, and her bedroom window broken. Hugh and I stood there, looking at each other, unable to express the blackness that has taken over our lives.

—Aoibheann

We met at Evelyn's at eight o'clock. Kate and Charlie's dad were in the hallway talking, waiting for the bathroom so that they could change into their robes.

Evelyn swished down the hall from the direction of the kitchen, elegant in a long purple robe with wide, sweeping sleeves. She had a beautiful silver pentacle around her neck. She came right for me, her face serene, and kissed my forehead. I noticed that stopped the conversation Kate and Sam had started. I don't think Charlie's dad noticed anything.

"Come with me for a minute, Alisa," Evelyn said, drawing me into the study and shutting the doors behind us.

On her desk there was a large, dusty old box. She walked around to it and opened the limp flaps at the top.

"It's time these saw the light of day again," she said, looking down into the contents. She seemed lost in whatever it was she was looking at; then she waved me over and pushed the box toward me.

"These are for you," she said.

Inside, there was a bundle of purple cloth. I had scried this! A box, something purple! Eagerly I opened the bundle. As I dipped my hand into the folds, I got a sharp spark of electricity and drew my hand back. Evelyn nodded for me to continue, so I reached in again. My hand hit something smooth and flat. I pulled it out. It was a ceramic plate, handmade—very seventies, crafty looking, with a pentagram thickly drawn into the surface. I reached in again and produced a chalice, silver, with a stem made of figures of the moon and stars. A chunk of quartz wrapped in yellow silk. A bolline—the white-handled work knife used to prepare herbs and other magickal elements. Many of these items sat in the small cauldron, which I had to pull out with both hands.

These were my mother's things. They warmed my hands as I touched them.

I looked up at Evelyn, unable to speak.

"There's something else," she said, nodding for me to reach in once again. At the bottom of the bundle there was a pale green linen robe, finely embroidered with runes.

"She made this by hand," said Evelyn, running her fingers over the embroidery. "Every stitch is sacred."

I picked it up, but it was surprisingly heavy. Something was wrapped inside. As I unfolded it, I saw a glint of metal. I drew in my breath in surprise.

"Does it look familiar?" Evelyn said, watching me with glistening eyes.

It was an athame with a bright silver blade. But my eyes were stuck on the handle. It was cast in the shape of a mermaid—a steel gray mermaid.

I ran my hand over the sculpted handle, tears welling up behind my eyes. The mermaid—this was what had been calling me here, and now I had it. The athame was beautiful, and it was my mother's. I imagined her holding it in her hand, wearing her light green robe as she worked some beautiful magick. Before the storm. Before everything changed for her. I looked back at Evelyn as a few tears began to slip down my face. "I can't believe it," I whispered.

"The Goddess often speaks to us in our dreams," she said.

*   *   *

Evelyn had instructed me to remove all of my clothing, even my underwear, before putting on the robe. I thought this would make me very cold, especially with those seaside breezes blowing all over the place, but I was comfortable in the fine linen. The fit was perfect—my mother and I must have been the exact same height. Standing there in my robe and holding the athame, my bare feet on the cool nighttime grass, I felt so witchy . . . and so natural.

The house had a large backyard, which I hadn't seen before. It was surrounded on all sides by trees, so we were in a safe little grotto for the circle. White lights had been strung around, making the scene romantic. The large cauldron contained a sweet-smelling fire, laced with herbs and fragrant woods. I took my place in the opening of the group, beside Sam, who looked quite dashing in his crimson silk robe. Charlie stood just opposite me, looking amazing in a pale yellow robe. He nodded slightly but approvingly in my direction.

Evelyn stepped forward and presented the four elements—the candle, the incense, the bowl of water, and the dish of sea salt.

"Alisa," she said, "if you would please bring out your athame, I would like you to cast the circle."

She held out the bowl of water and indicated that I should dip my athame in it. When I had done so, she placed the elements in their respective quarters and nodded for me to begin.

I'd never actually done this before, so I was a bit nervous. You're supposed to try to make the circle as perfectly round as possible. Using my right hand, I held the athame out in front of me. Walking deasil around the group, I concentrated on feeling its power, and I visualized the wall of energy that I was drawing. Automatically I started to speak, not really knowing where I had found the invocation. I supposed maybe I'd read it somewhere, but it came out of me naturally, as if I was saying my own name: "I conjure you, circle, to be a protected space, boring down through the earth and rising into the sky. I cast out from you all that is impure. Within your protective embrace, may we honor the Goddess and the God."

Evelyn smiled, and I took my place. I saw quite a number of surprised glances ping-ponging between Evelyn and me. The circle was very peaceful—no busted pipes, no floods. When it was over, everyone headed for a table that had been set up next to the house. There were cookies, brownies, and little bowls of milk and rosewater pudding decorated with rose petals. Someone switched on some Celtic music. I stayed with Sam most of the time, chatting with Kate—but I was really scanning the yard for Charlie. He had vanished into thin air the moment the circle was over.

When I was alone for a moment by the table, Brigid approached me, reaching past me for an oatcake. I felt a chilly, brittle energy coming from her.

"Hi," I said. "This circle—it was great. It was beautiful."

She picked through all of the cakes very deliberately before choosing one. At last she looked up at me. "You saved Charlie last night. Thank you."

I opened my mouth to respond but quickly realized that I had no idea what to say. I didn't feel like I should be accepting thanks for something like that. Finally I just nodded.

"I'm not happy about what's happened," she said, real sadness tearing at her voice, "but what you did was good."

Having said her piece, she walked off. I saw her go into the house.

"What happened?" I said out loud to no one in particular. I desperately wanted to find Charlie and ask, but his dad came up to me at that very moment.

"I've checked my schedule," he said. "I didn't have a few full days."

I had no idea what he was talking about. "I'm sorry?" I said.

"You asked me if I had a few days to listen to your story," he explained. "I do, but not until June. Maybe we could speak on the phone instead. I'd very much like to hear all about your experiences. Charlie's told me some, and I am absolutely fascinated."

"Oh." I laughed. "Right. Sure."

"Wonderful," he said, taking a dish of pudding. "Does Charlie have your phone number?"

"I'll give it to him," I replied. "Have you seen him?"

"Oh, yes," he said, peering around the yard. "He's on one of the benches in the back."

Far in the back of the yard, there was a small clump of four tall shrubs. In the middle of these was a tiny white stone bench, and on this bench was Charlie. As usual, my stomach twisted around completely.

"You found me," he said, sounding kind of pleased.

"I'm supposed to give you my phone number," I said, joining him on the bench.

"Oh, yeah?" he said, arching his brows.

"Your dad wants it."

"My dad's been asking for your number?" He laughed. "Is there something going on I should know about?"

I felt myself blushing. "Um, listen, I'm sorry about yester-day," I said. "I didn't mean ..."

"No." He shook his head quickly. "No! Don't apologize." He looked around and then checked his watch. "Let me explain, but not here. Can I give you a ride back to Sam's? Things are wrapping up here, anyway."

My ride arrangements were fine with Sam, so I went back inside to change into my clothes, and I carefully folded the robe and put it in with my mother's tools. Evelyn gave me a warm hug and another kiss on the forehead as I left.

"We have a lot of work to do," she said to me quietly. "We need to put these tools back to good use."

"Thank you ..." I said, not even sure how to express my gratitude.

"Call me Grandmother," she said with a smile. "That is my name. Or Grandmom. Gran. Whatever you like."

I'd only ever had one grandmother, and she was from Buenos Aires. I called her Lita Soto.

"How about Lita?" I asked. "It's a nickname for grand-mother in Spanish."

"I like it," she said with a satisfied nod. "I like it a lot."

18

The Castle

February 13, 1991

I sat straight up in bed at three o'clock this morning and screamed.

Poor Ruth, I think I scared her half to death. I woke little Brigid as well. They both turned up at my door. While I assured them that I had just had a bad dream, I knew it was more. My heart ached as though it were broken. It's difficult to explain, but it felt as though a candle that always burned inside me had been snuffed out. I felt an emptiness, an indescribable loss.

After Ruth and Brigid had gone back to bed, I walked all through the house, trying to convince myself that there was some reasonable explanation for my disturbance. I walked through the basement, the kitchen, and the study, praying to the Goddess that I would find some mundane solution. But in my heart I knew there would not be, and my heart was right.

In my workroom, Sorcha's old bedroom, I found everything in

a shambles. The shelves had collapsed, and everything I was storing had tumbled down. The carpet was shredded where the bed once stood. I knew then that my worst suspicions were true.

My daughter, my lost Sorcha, is dead.

—Aoibheann

Charlie guided the car through the streets of Gloucester, past the huge neon Gorton's fisherman and the crowded pubs along the waterfront. He didn't say anything at first— he just played with the windshield wipers, flicking them on and off, as if they could help him clear his thoughts. I couldn't get a good read on what he was feeling. It felt like a whole soup of emotions.

"On Monday," he finally said, "in the basement, I told Brigid what happened."

I remembered the wave of emotion I'd felt coming from Brigid as I passed—that whole nasty mix of panic, anger, and sadness. It made me nauseous just to think of it.

"You mean what happened in the library," I said.

"Right." He nodded. "And it was really bad. She was so upset. I've never done anything like that."

"I'm sorry," I said. "I've caused a mess. . . ."

"No!" he said, accidentally jerking the wheel a bit as he turned to look at me. "It's not that I regret it. I'm sorry I was so quiet yesterday. I was just trying to take care of things."

"Take care of things?" I asked.

"I spent yesterday thinking it all over," he continued. "Today I told her that I needed a little time to think things over."

"You . . . broke up with her?"

He stopped for a red light and turned to me. "Yes," he said. "I think so."

I nodded, unsure of what to say. I didn't think, "Great!" would be appropriate, but by now it was clear that we had some kind of bond, however strange and undefined.

"It's for the best," he said. "We've been together for two years, since she was fourteen. Now she's sixteen and I'm seventeen. I care about her a lot, but we've both grown and changed. I don't think we're the best match for each other." The light turned green, and he drove through the intersection. "I'm going off to college in the fall. I'm going to be leaving Gloucester." His tone was pained, as if he was trying to convince me and convince himself that he had done the right thing. He fell silent for a minute, obviously not sure what to say next.

"Evelyn and I had a talk, too," I said.

He pulled into a small parking lot and killed the engine.

"About what?" he said, unsnapping his seat belt and turning to me. "I mean, everything seemed good at the circle tonight. I was wondering what was going on."

While I didn't explain what had transpired in detail, I told him that Evelyn and I had reconciled, and I explained what had been in the box in the back.

"Alisa." He broke into a smile and took my hands. "That's great. I can't believe I didn't notice. . . . I'm sorry."

"It's all right," I said, smiling, too. "You had a lot on your mind. How do you feel?"

"Well," he said, "I feel like a jerk for what I've done to Brigid, even though I think it's for the best. And I feel incredibly happy that you're here."

He watched me to see what effect his words were

having. I'll tell you what effect they had—I almost melted. Kissing energy was on the rise.

"I wanted to show you this place," he said, pointing out into the shadows. "Take a look."

I leaned forward and glanced up through the windshield. Then I rubbed my eyes and looked again. It was a medieval castle—complete with turrets, drawbridge, the works. I wondered if he had spelled some kind of illusion.

"It's called Hammond Castle. It's real," Charlie said, answering my unspoken question. "Well, it's a real fake. It was built in the 1920s by a rich inventor. He wanted a nice place for his art collection."

"This is really strange," I said, "but cool." And absurdly romantic, of course.

"Over there," he said, pointing out into the inky darkness of the water, just past the castle, "is one of the most famous places along the shoreline. It's a rock called Norman's Woe, the site of many shipwrecks and the inspiration for the poem 'The Wreck of the Hesperus,' which I will now recite to you."

He drew himself up, as if he was about to give a big speech. I stared blankly.

"Just kidding," he said quickly, breaking into a grin. "But the force of the sea and the spirits of the sailors give this place tons of energy. It's our local power sink. I've per-formed some amazing magick here."

We got out of the car and sat down on a bench in a small stone bell tower, where we could hear the roar of the ocean just below. The floodlights illuminated the towers above us and threw strange shadows on the ground.

"Hold on," he said. He went back to his car and came back with his messenger bag.

"Want to learn a little spell?" he asked.

"As long as it doesn't make anything fall over or break," I said. "Or make my clothes disappear!"

"No." He laughed. "Nothing like that. This one brings back something that made you happy once, a good experience. Sometimes just something you like to eat or a beautiful sunset. It's a small spell, but it's a nice one. It reminds you of a joy in your life."

"That sounds nice," I said. "Sure. Show me."

He penciled the Gaelic on a slip of paper and went over the pronunciations with me. I practiced it a few times. After the dark wave spell this little three liner was nothing. Then he poured about a half cup of coarse sea salt into my hand.

"Okay," he said, "I'll draw the circle. You walk it deasil three times. Say one line each time you go around. After you recite the spell, close your eyes and throw this straight up in the air, right above your head. Get it all up there in one strong, fast throw. Keep facing up, letting it fall back down to you."

Taking some more of the salt, he drew a circle on the asphalt, leaving me a space to step inside. He closed it behind me. Then he drew sigils in the air, signifying the four elements. He nodded at me to begin. I made my three circles, reciting one line each time:

"Ar iobairt ar miann
an sòlas goit faod till
tromhad tràth-sa."

I closed my eyes, and with one swift stroke I threw the salt into the air. I was expecting it to rain back down on my head, but it never came. Instead, the snapping ocean breezes seemed to stop. I couldn't hear the waves hitting the shore, and I couldn't smell the salty air.

"What is this?" I said, suddenly panicking.

"Relax," I heard him say. "Just let it come. Close your eyes and breathe slowly."

Now the air felt warm to me, like a heady summer breeze or like every day in Texas, where I had been born. There were chirping cicadas. There was grass, soft grass high around my ankles. I felt unsteady, but a pair of strong hands were holding mine, stretching my arms above my head.

I smelled lilacs.

My mother. My mother was teaching me how to walk. She was taking me over to a pot of flowers. I started to run to them and lost my balance, but the hands caught me. I heard laughter. She was encouraging me.

"You've got it, Alisa," the voice was saying. Her voice. "Good girl. You did it."

I looked up, and I saw her. Her face was like mine.

"You did it," she repeated.

Encouraged, I took off again toward the flowers, but they faded from my view.

In a moment the sound of the ocean returned, and the wind kicked back up. The fragrance rose like a lifting fog and dissipated. I kept trying to breathe in more deeply, just to get one last breath. Different hands held me. Larger hands, with cooler skin and longer fingers that could grip my arms all the way around.

"Alisa!"

I opened my eyes. I had tipped forward, and Charlie had caught me before I went facedown on the ground. He said a blessing to close the circle and helped me over to the stone bench. As I watched him brush away the salt, my vision grew mistier. No magick this time—I was crying. He looked over in alarm.

"What did you see?" he asked, coming over and squatting down in front of me. I shook my head. I couldn't describe it.

"Was it something bad?" he said, his brow furrowed. "This is such a gentle spell. What . . . ?"

"It was my mother," I said.

He exhaled sharply and shook his head.

"Alisa," he said, "I'm sorry. We're at Norman's Woe. I should have realized that the spell would intensify. I'm an idiot."

"No," I said, wiping my eyes. "No. It was . . . good."

He sat down and took me in his arms. We listened to the waves hitting the shore just below us. Normally I would have been a complete wreck sitting there, wondering if he was going to kiss me again, worrying about what I should do or say. But my thoughts were on bigger matters, and Charlie seemed to understand that.

It was all clear to me now, what all of this had been about. I'd reconciled with my grandmother. I'd gotten the mermaid-handled athame and the rest of my mother's tools. I'd come to grips with my heritage. These were all the things my mother had been trying to show me.

Now, I realized, I could go home.

19

Full Circle

February 16, 1991

I haven't explained to anyone yet what I know to be true:
Sorcha is indeed gone. I have performed multiple divination
rituals, and the result is always the same.

Somhairle will take it very hard. He has never stopped
grieving for his lost sister, and I think he has always felt that
they would be reunited one day. It was not to be.

Some time ago Somhairle told me that he had received word that
Sorcha had a child, a baby girl named Alisa. The poor child is
without a mother now, only three years old. She will never know
the joy of magick, the indescribable feeling of being with the Goddess.
If only Sorcha had never left us, if only she had never turned her
back on her family or denied the beautiful powers given her by the
Goddess. Now this poor child will never know us and will never
discover the great richness of her Rowanwand heritage. I might have
had a beautiful, powerful granddaughter.

Now that is never to be.

—Aoibheann

"Sorry it's so late," I said sheepishly when I called Hunter. "You weren't in bed, were you?"

"No, not for hours yet," Hunter said. "How was the circle tonight?"

I'd arrived back at Sam's just moments before, and I had immediately picked up the phone. Not only did I owe Hunter a call, but I figured that once I told Hunter I was coming home, I couldn't back out. I had to move quickly before I lost my nerve.

"It was good," I said. "Different. My grandmother, she gave me my mother's tools. The athame . . . it has a mermaid handle."

Hunter gave a low whistle. He'd heard about my dream from Morgan.

"Oh," he said. "I see."

"At least I know I wasn't crazy," I said.

"I never thought you were crazy," he said matter-of-factly.

"I did," I said with a laugh. "Plenty of times. But Hunter . . . I . . ."

"Yes?"

"I know I need to come home, as soon as possible."

"That would probably be for the best," Hunter said, his voice immediately getting very calm. "The longer you wait, the more problems you may have."

"Maybe there's a bus leaving tonight," I replied, looking around the room as if I thought Sam would have a huge bus schedule on the wall.

"No, not the bus. I'll come get you," he said, in a tone that didn't suggest I had an option.

I thought of what was probably a four-hour trip each way.

"Hunter, it's far. You don't have to . . ."

"I know I don't have to. I want to. I'll leave soon. Tell me exactly where you are."

After listening to me make rambling guesses about the driving directions for about five minutes, Hunter cleared his throat and politely interrupted me. "That's all right," he said. "I'll find the best route to Gloucester on a map. The sigil will guide me from there."

"How will I know when you're coming?" I said. "Should I set an alarm?"

"No need," he said. "You'll know. The sigil will warn you."

"Hunter . . . um, thanks. For everything. For what you did the other night—for this. There was a lot I needed to deal with."

He didn't reply for a second.

"I'm pleased to help," he said, his voice softening. "And Alisa, I'm glad you found what you were looking for."

We got off soon after. There would be plenty of time for me to tell him everything on the long car ride home. I readied myself for a second call. Sam had Charlie's number in his little phone book on the counter. When he answered, I could hear music in the background. He seemed excited that I had called so soon after he dropped me off. But then he seemed to pick up on something, maybe the tone of my voice.

"Something's up," he said.

"Yeah," I said sadly.

"It's not great news," he said, "is it?"

"I have to go home. I have to go back to my family."

"When?"

"Tomorrow morning."

I heard the springs as he sat down quickly on his bed.

"Do I smell or something?" he said, trying to make his voice sound light. "Because I'll shower . . ."

"I'm sorry. I'd really like to stay, but I have to go before the situation at home gets worse than it already is. My dad is really upset."

"A runaway." He sighed. "A fugitive. I fell for a dangerous type."

Fell for. Charlie had fallen for me. No one fell for me. I fell—into things, over things. I caused things to fall over. But no one had fallen for me, until now. I sank into one of the kitchen chairs, fighting the urge to call Hunter back and tell him not to come.

"But," Charlie went on, "it makes sense. You don't want to mess up your life. As much as I hate the thought of your leaving, it's better that you should go. I don't want you to end up locked in your house until you're ninety-five."

"If that happens," I replied, "you'll come and bust me out, right?"

"Of course!" he said. "But for now, I'll drive you home. I could get the day off, no problem."

I'd always thought it was a cliché, but I actually got but-terflies in my stomach at the thought of being alone with Charlie in a car for four hours. But my head knew that it wasn't a great idea. "Um, well, my coven leader is going to pick me up," I said reluctantly. "Believe me, it's better that way. It'll be difficult when I get home. That's not the way I'd like you to meet my dad."

The music in the background was the only noise I heard for a minute.

"You'll be in touch," he said, "right?"

"I'll annoy you with e-mail," I said. "I promise. You'll be *so* sick of me."

"I'd better be," he said. I could hear that he had smiled as he said that. "I want full reports on the whole Hilary situation."

"Oh," I said, "don't worry about that. You'll get those. The big wedding is coming up all too soon."

Neither one of us could figure out how to get off the phone, so we talked for a few more minutes, both of us trying to sound casual. Being Charlie, he had to crack a few jokes about how he had chased me away. Being me, I had to sniffle a lot. He promised to come and visit New York as soon as he could.

Just one more gut-wrenching conversation to go.

Sam was sitting up in his bed, reading, when I knocked. He welcomed me in. His bedroom was gorgeous. Very Sam. The furniture was huge and antique, with dragonfly-patterned stained-glass lamps on either side of the bed. The cats were contentedly nuzzling each other. I sat down on his down comforter near the foot of the bed.

"I have to go home," I said, stroking Mandu as he came up and stood on my lap. "My coven leader is coming for me. He'll be here in the morning, probably pretty early."

Sam set down his book and took off his glasses.

"Tomorrow morning?" he repeated.

I nodded.

"Good luck, Alisa," he said gently, reaching over to take my hand. "I'm not going to say good-bye, because I know you'll be back. The door is always open here."

"Thanks," I said, going all misty once again. These good-byes were rough. I could see that his eyes were getting red as well. I sat there for a few moments, petting the cats, just taking in the moment with Sam.

"You're tired," he finally said, looking me in the eye. "It's time you got some sleep."

He was right. I was exhausted, but I was also too edgy to rest. Sam got up and walked me back downstairs, his arm over my shoulders. After he had securely tucked me into my bed on the couch, he put his hand to my forehead, and I felt a slow, blissful relaxation take me over. It felt like I was lying on a raft in a pool, the lulling bump of the water pushing me along inch by inch. I was asleep within seconds. I don't even remember Sam turning out the light or going back upstairs, so I have no idea how long he sat there.

I had another dream that night, but it wasn't like the one about the mermaid. I was back in the yard with my mother, walking toward the pot of flowers. Once again I looked up, but this time I could see her clearly. I saw the almond shape of her eyes, so much like mine. Her pale skin was flushed by the Texas sun.

"You did it," she said again.

Then I realized—I wasn't a toddler. It was me, just as I am now, standing across from her and holding her hands.

"You showed me," I managed to say.

She shook her head and said no more. But her smile told me everything.